Confessions of a Jihadist

By
Ponmala

Vitasta
Let Knowledge Spread

Published by
Renu Kaul Verma
Vitasta Publishing Pvt Ltd
2/15, Ansari Road, Daryaganj
New Delhi - 110 002
info@vitastapublishing.com

ISBN 978-93-82711-77-3

Typeset and Cover Design by Vits Press
Printed by Vikas Computer and Printers

Contents

A Total Solar Eclipse	1
Pandit Shingdi	16
The Party	43
The Hidden Treasure	68
Satsang Baba	95
Border Dispute	124
Bumbum Raja Bumbum Rani	154
Love In Paradise	181
At The Threshold Of Hell	195
The Call Of Jihad	211

To Saly

Chapter - 1

A Total Solar Eclipse

I have a wife.

She is wonderful—for me.

And if you have functional testicles, I wouldn't want you to think she is wonderful.

If you insist that you will, I'll break your bones. And if you are stronger than I, I'll call my son for help. He's just got a yellow belt.

And, I repeat, my wife is a wonderful creature, definitely more wonderful than your wife, if you have one. Don't think I am belittling other people's wives. I am only safeguarding the integrity of my bones.

And I assert for the third time that my wife is a wonderful woman… I feel reassured now. My wife is indeed wonderful.

Want to know what is so wonderful about my wife?

Here's the answer.

Variety is the spice of life, and my wife is variety personified. I will showcase one charming aspect of her, her colour, and elucidate the point.

She is a chameleon. She changes colours according to the seasons, weather, intensity of daylight, the shape of the moon, her moods etc etc. She is never monotonous. She keeps me ever youthful, because my life moves on from romance to romance, falling in love with her every new avatar.

There is variety even in the exposed parts of her body. Her face is fair—by Indians standards; her hands, feet and midriff are dusky; her neck and a five-inch semicircle down the neck, both in front and back, are darker than fair and fairer than dusky.

She once had enchanting cat-eyes. Now they are normal South Indian eyes.

Her hair was light brown when I married her, but now they appear grey.

Unlike other people's wives, she is fairer when she growls and darker when she smiles and yields to me, which she does usually after it gets very dark. I'll not tell you what her colour is when I hold her, like in the moments when God gave us our two children.

She wasn't always a chameleon; she was monochrome

when I first met her. She was fair all over—and covered all over. It was our dramatic first encounter that turned her into a chameleon. And that's the story I want to tell you. It's the story about how she became the bone of my bones and the flesh of my flesh.

That day, the sun set at three past three in the afternoon. Birds flew to their nests and men withdrew to their houses. *Pujari*s sat in front of idols and chanted mantras, and pregnant women offered their prayers in the darkest recesses of their houses, pouring milk on *Shiv Lingas*. Just a few men and children looked into plates, filled with cow dung mixed water and placed in the open. There was an eerie silence. A total solar eclipse was on.

I was travelling in a suburban train, unconcerned about the ominous spectacle during which the heavens emptied their evil dredge onto the world. A beggar and I were the only occupants of the car that I later boarded. Everyone had taken precaution against the ill-effects of the sun's disappearance into the mouth of a demon and remained homebound, I had not. And I was to pay the price for it—or, rather, be rewarded with a prize catch, as events would ultimately prove.

I was heading for a very crowded part of the city where one Mr Sreenat lived, who possessed a secret *ayurvedic* medicine that dissolved kidney stones. I wanted the medicine for a distant cousin of my mother. Locating the man's house, I knew, would be a tough hunt.

I had gone there once to meet a friend. The place was a jungle of identical medieval houses, joining hands against the ravages of time to which they would succumb any day. One would need the help of a guide to locate a house. My friend, who had his house there, had promised to wait for me at the nearest railway station.

I detrained twenty minutes after the demon had vomited the sun out and the city had started pouring into the streets. My friend did not turn up at the railway station. His wife had prevented him from stepping out of the house on a solar eclipse day. I, therefore, took a risk and went in search of Mr Sreenat's house on foot. I got lost in a labyrinth of narrow lanes that seemed to interconnect with the devilish design of trapping any stranger who ventured on to them. There were ready helps like 'go a little further, take a left turn and walk for five minutes along the right diversion where anyone you ask will show you Mr Sreenat's house' which made me go round and round. I bore the anger of a disgraced sun for an hour.

Finally my weary legs and sweat-soaked clothes forced me to sit for a while on a debris heap.

A sympathetic old man came by.

"What ails you, son?" he asked.

"I'm okay. I got tired searching for a house."

"Whose house?"

"Mr Sreenat's, the man who gives medicine for kidney stones. I have been searching for his house all the way from the railway station."

"You have come too far, son. Sreenat's house is near the railway station. You will have to walk back almost three kilometres."

I nearly passed out.

It was the concern for my mother's distant cousin, who was in agony because of the stones his kidneys had swallowed, that restored my vigour. I raised myself up from the debris heap and walked in the reverse direction. When I looked up, I saw the clouds keeping back at the outer edges of the sky, frightened off by the sun's angry growls. I dared to sweat it out.

I came to the vicinity of Mr Sreenat's house at last.

"The third house there," a young boy pointed out, stretching out his hand to the right.

I reached the house, stood in the front verandah and pressed the bell-push. A window opened and a lovely face of a woman appeared. Two cat-eyes fell on my face and instantly the horror of an atomic explosion overtook them. The window was slammed shut.

"Get away! Get away!" I heard the woman shriek hysterically.

'What was the matter!'

I feared that an exposure to the solar eclipse had turned my face into that of a Dracula. I passed trembling hands over my face. I could feel folds and deep furrows.

"Get away! Get away!" I heard the woman scream again.

I took to my heels, but fear unbalanced me. I was tottering away when some men rushed towards me. Something hit my head hard.

I will cut a long story short. One of the men who rushed in hearing the woman scream hit my head with an iron rod. I slumped to the ground unconscious. Luckily, my friend who had failed to turn up at the railway station was among those who converged on me. His timely intervention saved me from more thrashing. He rushed me to a hospital. The doctors made a thorough and costly investigation and came to the conclusion that my brain had suffered no serious damage. There was a two-inch cut on my scalp, which the doctors sutured up. I was advised to stay at the hospital for a day, in case there was some damage which their investigation had missed and would cause a crisis. My friend attended to me. I was in an alien city and had no relatives who could rush to my help.

I must mention a couple of things I missed. I had misjudged the direction the boy pointed to. I went to the house towards which his hand was stretched. I now remember his forefinger was bent in the opposite direction. I had got fooled by the prank. Mr Sreenat's house was directly opposite to the one where the misfortune befell me. The second thing I should mention is that I looked into a mirror as soon as I reached the hospital and was relieved to find that the solar eclipse had not distorted my face.

"You have landed the woman in great trouble," my friend accused.

"But what wrong have I done? I didn't speak a word to her. She became hysteric and screamed the moment she saw me."

"But you saw her, didn't you?"

"What of that?"

"Your eyes defiled her. She is now a sullied woman."

My friend impressed on me that I had committed a great blunder. He wouldn't give ear to my protest that I might have at worst committed a misdemeanour by entering the verandah and ringing the call bell of a house where a veiled woman lived— describing her the way she appeared to the outside world. He explained to me that the woman had looked out thinking that her husband or maid servant had rung the bell. It was a fatal error for which she immediately paid a heavy price. She was married to a sheikh who had come holidaying to India. The man was concluding his holidays. On the pretext that the gaze of a stranger had defiled his wife of two months, he pronounced the triple *talaq* on her and caught the next flight home where a nestful of undefiled wives were longing for his return.

My friend went on repeating his accusation that my thoughtlessness had ruined a woman till the gravity of my crime sunk in and I agreed for a reparation by accepting the woman as my wife. I agreed to all her terms, the most serious of which were that she would continue to wear the veil whenever she stepped out of the house and that I should agree to a minor alteration to one of my organs, the name of which my wife does not allow me to mention.

In the euphoria of our first night, I also murmured one sweet promise into her ear: I would under no circumstance pronounce the triple *talaq* on her till the next total solar eclipse.

My marriage to Shakeela has outlived two total solar eclipses, one happily and another rather bitterly.

But my story does not end there. When I allowed my wife to continue to wear the veil, I had also resolved that I would, step by step, coax her to discard it.

My first chance for it came four months later, on the day I received the photos of our visit to the monument of love, the Taj Mahal. I showed them to her.

"You shouldn't have got the photos taken," she protested.

"Why?"

"Because I don't want to have my photo taken. They might get into the hands of some stranger one day. I don't want any random stranger to gaze at my photos. Destroy them!"

"They are not your photos."

"Don't fool me."

"I'm not fooling you. I'm telling you the truth. How can you claim you are in these photos?"

"Because I am in them."

"Where?"

"By your side."

"How can you say it's you? It could as well be any other woman. In fact, the woman by my side is a call girl. See how easily she could replace you when she covered herself with a veil."

This let loose a tantrum from her. Plates splintered, chairs got maimed, cushions were knifed and we went without food for a whole day.

The next day hunger withered her and it made me cringe. We came to talking terms.

"You're right, darling, the woman in the photos is you. I was just fooling."

"I don't believe you."

I placed my hands on her tummy. She was two months pregnant.

"I swear by our child the woman is you. I was just trying

to put across to you the point that I can so easily cheat you if you hide yourself within a veil from the world all your life. This veil is doing terrible injustice to you and to me. Except for God, me and a few of your kin, you don't exist."

"That's all I want. It's enough that the world hears of me as your wife now and the mother of your children in the future."

"That's not enough, dear. The eyes and the face identify an individual. Please discard at least the piece that covers your face. You will then become a person who can be identified in a crowd. I can identify my wife to others and our children will be able to recognise their mother."

"The devil has got into your brain."

"Believe me, darling, the time is not far when we will see robotised test-tubes carrying children walk on our streets in the appearance of comely women. And if they will wear veils, for which I am sure someone will issue an edict, you will just pass off as one of them in their company."

She got into a tantrum once again. More plates broke, more chairs got maimed, more cushions were knifed, and we went without food for two days.

Leghorns were a new wonder then. I took my wife one day to a big farm which maintained twenty thousand of the chicken that laid a large number of eggs. The birds were housed in small symmetrical cages built in long rows. The cages had just sufficient space for them to stand. They serried like disciplined soldiers and operated like automatic machines that pecked food all the while and laid eggs once a day.

"What cruelty is this!" my wife shouted. "They have packed the birds in cages like lifeless things. The sight makes me feel sick. Why did you bring me here? Let's go."

"It's the same sickening feeling that I have when I see you in the veil," I said.

Thankfully, we were not at home. So, plates did not splinter, chairs did not get maimed and cushions were not knifed, but we went without food for three days.

Then, early in the fourth morning, she woke me up with a loving caress. Strangely, she was wearing the veil. She was going to hide herself in the veil at home too to teach me a lesson. I hid my face away in protest.

In the evening, she tickled me till I looked at her. She had made two holes in her veil which revealed just her eyes. It was a frightening sight. But it still gladdened me, because I had broken the ice.

Then a terrible thing happened, which I thought would force Shakeela to at least uncover her face. A girl went out of her mind when she saw two large catlike eyes approach her in the dark— the girl is still under psychiatric treatment. But even that did nothing to shake her complete commitment to the totality of the veil.

And just when I decided to wave a white flag, realising

that the battle against the veil was pushing me into a nervous breakdown, I got a brilliant flash suggesting a final assault that looked promising. It was a cerebral argument on the injustice that the full veil represented. I asked her, "You see everyone while you hide your face from everyone; is that just?"

"Ask the others to wear a veil and hide their face from me. I have no objection," she replied curtly.

"How do you think the world would be like if everyone covers himself or herself head to toe in a veil? Would you want to live in such a world?" I questioned.

Her answer to it was a sneering glower.

I pressed on, "Justice demands that you blindfold yourself when you walk out in a full veil. If you are a truly upright woman who believes in a just God, you'll do so."

She stormed out, banging the door shut behind her. But it worked; she removed the piece that covered her face when we went out that evening.

By our first wedding anniversary, I had coaxed my wife to discard the veil altogether, revealing her midriff and the dazzling saris for which I had spent a fortune. She was no more just the wife of Shreeman. She was Shakeela. She had her own slot in the world.

I had climbed Everest!

The world envied me. Word got around that people born under certain stars could get beautiful wives if they exposed themselves to a total solar eclipse. Some envious friends gave the sly suggestion that I should get Shakeela back into the veil to preserve her beauty. I greatly enjoyed the envy.

My first child, a daughter, brought me great luck. I got a well-paid job at a multinational company. I bought an apartment in a newly developed part of the city, adjacent to a large market complex, completed but unoccupied. We shifted to the new apartment immediately after our daughter had learnt to break into a run.

The first VIP guests we received in our apartment were two young women, both employees of the company I was working for. They were on a fact-finding mission in India from the headquarters of my employer. They were zealous feminists who believed that women would be truly feminine only if they aped men in everything. They wanted to see and verify my claim that I had succeeded in coaxing my wife into discarding the veil.

Shakeela and I wanted to make an impression when the fair-skinned feminists visited us. We had to buy new plates, new chairs and new cushions. We also had to buy a TV. We did not have one. Shakeela would not allow me bring the 'devil box' into the house. She was in a way justified. The first thing she saw on the TV when we went to buy one was a war reportage. The camera was passing over macabre scenes of mutilated bodies. It lingered long on the body of a young woman whose upper half was fully exposed. It moved on but kept returning now and again to the exposed part of the dead woman.

"The devils exploit even a naked corpse," Shakeela scowled, and stormed out of the shop. I did not dare to explain to her then that sound economics forced TV channels to stoop so low. But in the liberated mood that was hers without the veil now, she acquiesced to buy a TV. I was overjoyed. It did not matter that I had to borrow money for making the purchase.

The visit of the two guests had imposed one more daunting task on us. The compound of the adjacent market complex had turned into an open latrine. The complaints the apartment residents made to the authorities had fallen on deaf ears. For a week, Shakeela and I took turns to throw stones at the squatters from our apartment. Our effort proved fruitful. We were saved from the embarrassment of our VIP guests watching a shitting *dharna* from our apartment.

I taught Shakeela how to serve VIP guests food. We prepared food taking care to avoid pungent spices. I instructed her in mannerisms that would please or hurt our guests' feminist ardour. In the end, we greatly impressed our guests with our hospitality. They were so charmed that, while taking leave, one of them forgot to take a folder she had brought along.

The next day we went with the folder to the hotel room where our guests were staying. Only one of them could be seen.

"Please be seated, Sherin is having a wash," the woman, dressed as scantily as a woman could, said.

Shakeela was already frowning. I kept my eyes off our host not to irritate her further. Our host tried to engage us in a conversation. Shakeela was in no mood to respond at all. I responded with closed eyes. The painful suspense was brought to an end by the explosive appearance of the other woman, Sherin, out of the bath in her birthday suit. On seeing us, she covered just her most feminine part with the towel she was holding. She approached and stood in front of us, smiling coolly. Shakeela screamed and stormed out. I mumbled something and handed the folder over to the almost naked host. I suffered a blackout.

I was out on the road when I came to my senses. I searched for Shakeela. She was nowhere to be found.

I believed Shakeela would have made for home and so I rushed there. The sight that awaited me at home was even more shocking than my first encounter with Shakeela. She was back in the veil!

Chapter - 2

Pandit Shingdi

Shakeela's sense of smell is clearly out of the ordinary. It lies outside the limits of humans, but I wouldn't call it supernatural. It would be more appropriate to call it subhuman—her sense of smell is more akin to that of a sniffer dog—but I shall not describe it so, because I am more interested in not displeasing my wife than in sticking to the accuracy of facts. She recognises the weakest, farthest and weirdest of smells. They affect her so profoundly that I have often misunderstood her to be cranky when she would suddenly take deep breaths and get lost in ecstasy, or pinch her nostrils, or start vomiting, for no apparent reason. It took me some time to realise that she was just normally reacting to her abnormal sense of smell.

But like all things extraordinary, Shakeela's keen nostrils also caused a fair share of troubles. Once, in the third month of our marriage, she suddenly retched and vomited while we were strolling in the city's most beautiful park.

"What stench has cut through this fragrant air and sickened you, honey?" I asked, rubbing down her back.

"It's not the stench. It's something more serious."

Something more serious! I got the fright of my life. Had she hidden from me that she was suffering some serious illness? Anything fatal? The solar eclipse was haunting me once again.

"What's it, honey?"

"I retched once this morning."

"Oh God! Why didn't you tell me that?" I took her to a nearby garden bench and seated her on it. "We shall go to a doctor."

"There is no need of that. There is nothing to fear about. Such things are normal after marriage."

What did that mean? During the past three months, a number of mysterious consequences of marriage had cropped up and confounded me, but none was as strange as vomiting. When would my turn for vomiting come? I sat close to her and wrapped my left arm around her. I was going to insist that I would fetch a taxi to take her to a doctor when she rested her head on my lap and flashed a coy smile.

"We are going to have a son," she said.

ꩠꩡꩠꩡ

Shakeela brought forth a daughter instead of a son in less than nine months and I ignored her miscalculations. In effect, the baby was a son. She came out with clenched fists, which I consider the mark of a man, and refused to repent and cry for the pain she had caused her mother, which again, I consider a manly trait. Not till the doctor held her upside down by her feet and smacked her thrice on her buttocks did she oblige with a whimper and indicate that she satisfied all the parameters of a healthy child. I had paid a special fee and got a stopwatch-armed assistant stationed in the labour room to record the exact time of her emergence out of her mother's womb to a hundredth-of-a-second accuracy. She was born one-twenty-fourth of a second after midnight.

The first thing I did after my daughter's birth was to rush to an astrologer.

"You and your wife are really lucky," the astrologer said. "Your daughter has escaped the evil effects of the most inauspicious new moon of the century by the minutest fraction of a second. You did the right thing by stationing an attendant with a stopwatch in the labour room. My predictions would have gone awfully off-track otherwise. A dim shadow of the new moon still covers her. It will linger on throughout her childhood. The permanent effect of it on her is that she will exhibit a man's temperament all her life. Do not ever tell anyone that she is born under a star that has predominantly male characteristics. You could jeopardise her chance of getting a match when she grows up."

I agreed. I haven't divulged the name of her star till now, and I am not going to do it now to satisfy your curiosity. Don't try to guess. She was not born under *Moolam*.

To this very moment, our daughter has been true to her manly traits and it has served my purpose right, as you will soon know. Her clenched-fist ardour to overthrow whatever she disliked steadily increased as she grew up.

I am indebted to my daughter for inheriting my dislike for the veil, which suddenly erupted while we were on our way to a wedding reception when she was a one-and-a-half-year-old. The little one started crying as we entered a crowded part of the city. Shakeela immediately took out the feeding bottle and thrust its nipple in the babe's mouth. The babe refused to suck the rubber nipple and, instead, frantically sought her mother's nipples, which were hiding under many layers, the outermost of which was the adamant veil. The child got frustrated when her two tender hands could not help its mouth get to the object of their quest. She bawled and thrashed about in her mother's lap. The bike was getting out of my control and it almost hit against a car. I swerved to the road margin and brought the bike to a halt. We dismounted.

"Feed the child, Shakeela, I shall stand as cover," I said, standing close in front of my wife.

"I'll have to remove the veil."

"Do it."

"I won't."

"How will we then manage the baby? She is dead hungry."

"If she is dead hungry, she'll suck the bottle. She's just being adamant like you. It's not good for a girl." Shakeela thrust the bottle's nipple again into the babe's mouth.

True to her star, my daughter refused to suck. Shakeela whacked her repeatedly. The baby bawled louder and louder. As the battle between a furious mother and her rebellious daughter shook the earth, something most unexpected happened—the little one wriggled out of her mother's hands and slipped down on to the muddy road margin. It rolled on the ground. I struggled to pick her up, but I could not get my grip on her. People gathered, and within seconds, a crowd encircled us.

"The baby is possessed," one said. "It must be the Holy Mother."

"It truly is so," another said. "The baby is rolling in circles. Only those possessed by the Holy Mother roll in circles."

Someone started a *bhajan* and the crowd joined in, clapping hands and shaking heads in unison. Our daughter continued her tantrum in a rhythmic roll.

What the hell was happening! When would the Holy Mother leave our child? The wedding we had to attend was no more in my mind; we would not reach in time.

Then the unexpected happened. Shakeela removed her veil. Our daughter immediately lay still. Shakeela lifted her and suckled her. The crowd dispersed.

What motherly love!

My daughter had accomplished what I had abandoned as an impossible task—she had forced Shakeela out of the veil. But I stopped bragging about it after a year, when my turn came to be subjugated by the power of her star.

The elf got into her head that day to irritate me by jumping from a windowsill to our springy bed, not once, twice or thrice, but as many times as I ordered her not to. Then I realised that such rebellion was not good for a girl. So I went into the kitchen and drew out a tender stick from a broom and beat her with it, not once, twice or thrice, but as many times as she jumped. Many broomsticks broke, but I could not break my daughter. She didn't cry, but I cried in the end. I continued to break sticks, because I wouldn't accept that I was a man born under a star having predominant female characteristics.

Finally, my wife intervened and saved me from the ultimate humiliation of utter defeat. She snatched the child away and locked herself with her in another room. I heard Shakeela drill the value of obedience in the tiny tot. I felt guilty and silly. I had thrashed my little daughter brutally just to prove that I was a man and she a girl, despite knowing that she was a helpless victim of her star.

I went out and bought a dozen lollipops, all of my daughter's favourite colour, green. When I returned with the lollipops, the mother and the child were playing happily. As soon as I showed the lollipops, my daughter leapt into my arms. She laughed and played with me as though nothing had happened between us. I examined her legs. There were ruddy stripes of weal all over. The sight forced me to tears. "Don't cry, papa," my daughter said, wiping my tears with her tiny fingers. I cuddled her and covered her with kisses.

We forgot the agony we went through because of the battle of the stars and started playing. Then, suddenly, she ran to the windowsill and clambered on to it. She stood smiling, ready to jump on to the cot. "Come with the stick, papa," she said, "I am going to jump on to the cot." Shakeela and I broke into laughter. Our daughter too joined in. Laughter shook our apartment. I never took the stick again.

Two years after Shakeela abandoned the veil for the second time, she became pregnant for the second time. As her day approached, there were clear signs that she was going to bring forth a son—she vomited more often than in the case of my daughter, felt weaker, her tummy was more bulgy towards the left. This time around I wanted to make sure that nothing like the shadow of the new moon affected my second child. I made enquiries if modern medical advancements could help my wife deliver the child at a fixed time within the last week of the expected date. The gynaecologist whom Shakeela was consulting told me that my child could be brought out into the world at the exact moment I chose, provided I agreed to my wife undergoing a caesarean delivery. Armed with the good news, I consulted eminent astrologer Sampat Iyer. I was lucky there again. Just three days before Shakeela's due date, there was a confluence of stars that drafts the horoscope of world conquerors, which happens only once in a millennium. The desire to bring forth a world conqueror made Shakeela agree to a caesarean.

The stopwatch came in handy again. The gynaecologist cut Shakeela's tummy and kept it open, watching intently at the stopwatch. She took our son out at the exact moment that would make him a world conqueror.

Our son is yet to conquer the world, but he has taken the first step towards that great destiny. He has conquered our home. He makes sure that his likes, commands, will and voice prevail at our home. He is a despot, but I can assure you the world will be a happier place under his rule – he is a loveable despot. Do not seek our daughter's opinion about it; she has not taken kindly to his replacing her as the despot of the house. (Sampat Iyer continues to remind me whenever I meet him that till the day our son becomes a world conqueror, we cannot be sure that the stopwatch has correctly recorded the time of his birth.)

Children often fight. It's so normal that it would not be normal to state it. And yet, I had not known that children fought so ferociously, especially when they were brother and sister. My children still carry indelible marks of their childhood battles. There are still scars of scratches on their faces. (My daughter has vowed that if the scars don't disappear in another two years when she will enter college, she will break the ceasefire I had brokered five years ago.) The strength of my son's canines is permanently reduced by two. There is a bald patch on my daughter's head where new hairs haven't come up after her brother pulled the old ones. The girl, fortunately, hasn't taken the loss seriously, thanks to the abundant hair she has inherited from me. But the fight in which she lost the tuft of hair almost caused a grave mishap. The tussle for a new eraser flared into a big fight. Agonized, after her hairs were pulled, my daughter ran into the kitchen, snatched a knife and flung it at her persecutor. The knife scraped past the target's ear, chopping a piece off it, and created the conditions for my brokering the ceasefire.

The ceasefire brought a halt to our children's fierce fights and would have made our home a dull place had not Shakeela and I started our fights over the children immediately thereafter. When the children made it a habit to forgive and forget, we felt uneasy and started taking sides and fighting on their behalf. More often than not, Shakeela took the side of our son and me of our daughter.

Shakeela had the vainglorious airs of the mother of a world conqueror. She wouldn't at all allow me to take the boy to task. She always intervened saying that I had no right to question a would-be world conquer. What I found unbearable was that, while we were willing to concede that she was the mother of a would-be world conqueror, she was not willing to concede that I was a would-be world conqueror's father and our daughter was a would-be world conqueror's sister. The proxy war became so serious that we became a terrible nuisance to our neighbours. One of them, Mr. Murari, my next door neighbour, finally made that known to us.

"Shreeman, I consider myself fortunate to have you as my neighbour," he said. "You and your wife are such nice people and your children are such lovely kids."

"Thank you so much for your compliment," I responded.

"I promise we shall strive to be worthy of your high regards in the future also."

"I was going to tell you that I find it inexplicable why there is always a fight going on in your house. I suggest you consult an astrologer. When good people are involved in interminable fights, it means there is incompatibility among their stars. The problem can only be solved with the help of an expert astrologer. I can suggest one if you want."

I felt humiliated. I had the feeling that my nearest neighbour was representing all the residents of our complex. I hadn't the least idea that the fights in my house had taken on such hellish proportions as to require the intervention of an astrologer. It was as bad as us getting packed in a cage and driven to an asylum by our neighbours but it would have been too risky not to accept his suggestion.

"Your reluctance is understandable," my neighbour pressed on, misinterpreting the reason for my rueful pause. "There's so vast a prevalence of superstitious prejudice against astrology in the world that it has become a fashion to denigrate it. I have no doubt that all the chaos in the world will get halved the moment half the world accepts the power of astrology to solve the problems every living thing faces. I know cases of scores of households where family members were always on each other till they had recourse to the service of an astrologer."

"I have no prejudices. I am an ardent fan of astrology. I am a regular consultee of Sampat Iyer."

"You have got the right man. Call him tomorrow. He will correctly diagnose the incompatibilities of your stars and prescribe the correct remedies. Peace will return to your home within hours."

Sampat Iyer understood the seriousness of the crisis I was facing and rushed to my house straightaway, postponing an appointment he had with the Minister of Excise who wanted to consult him if he could accept bribes after sunset on Fridays, the day of Laxmi, the goddess of wealth. A detailed study of the stars of the four of us twice over did not reveal any serious incompatibility that should have occasioned so hellish a situation in our house. It was then that our cat appeared on the scene.

"Is that your cat?" Sampat Iyer questioned.

"Yes," I answered.

"Do you keep any other animal as pet?"

"We also have a parakeet."

"Can it speak?"

"Not in any language that we can understand."

"Pets are good fun," Sampat Iyer said, "but few people realise that pets born under certain stars that don't suit a household, can create terrible problems. Never buy a pet without consulting about its stars. Do you know under which stars the cat and the parakeet were born?"

"We have absolutely no idea."

"That's quite natural," he said. "There is no astrologer who keeps a tab on the time when eggs hatch or animals litter. So the solution we suggest in situations such as this is to get rid of all pets from the house."

"I'll keep my cat," my daughter declared. "If you chase it away, I'll run away with it."

"I'll keep my parakeet," my son declared. "If you chase it away, I'll fly away with it."

Sampat Iyer knew child psychology well, and so did not exhibit any displeasure at our children's rebellious reaction. Instead, he suggested that we go on a long pilgrimage that should take us to at least seven holy places across the length and breadth of the country to cancel out the ill effects that the stars of the pets were having on our family. He also emphasised that we should undertake the pilgrimage within three weeks for it to be effective. Shakeela and the children jumped on to the solution. The financial burden of the pilgrimage made me speechless.

When I paid Sampat Iyer his fees, he secretly told me in the presence of Mr Murari that the surest way to bring peace into our house was to get rid of the pets. The pilgrimage would only be a chancy alternative; It works on God's pleasure.

ഉണ്ടാ

"Which holy places shall we visit," Shakeela asked as soon as we got into bed that night.

"I leave the choice to you," I replied. "Choose seven holy places within the city."

"Sampat Iyer specially mentioned that we must go to seven holy places across the length and breadth of the country."

"The capital represents the country just the way the head represents the individual. Before he left, I consulted Sampat Iyer on the astrological validity of this interpretation and got his approval."

"Did he say it would be wrong to interpret that the whole body represents the individual?"

"How could he say that?"

"Then what's wrong in going on a nationwide pilgrimage?"

"Don't you understand that so elaborate a pilgrimage is beyond the capacity of my purse?"

"Haven't you always brought up some such lame excuse whenever the children or I talked of a tour?"

"When was it that I could afford and I still refused?"

"When was it that you couldn't afford whatever you liked? When you wanted a TV, didn't you take a loan? What better purpose did it serve than making our children always fight for their choice channels? Why are you so allergic about religious matters? And you think there will be peace in the house without God's help?"

"Who told you I am not interested in religious matters? Don't I pray five times a day and recite the Quran daily? Who says longer pilgrimages are more effective than shorter pilgrimages? Why don't you realise that Allah will punish us if we take a loan to pay him visits? Hasn't Allah said paying interest is a sin?"

Our children banged at our door. They continued banging until I opened the door.

"Won't you stop hurling questions at each other?" my son shouted, staring furiously into my eyes.

"Aren't you whetting your appetite for a fight by shooting endless questions at each other? Won't you get sleep until you have a fight?" our daughter yelled, devouring me with her eyes.

I was already whetted sharp for a fight. I couldn't control myself.

"Who the hell are you to question me?" I bellowed at the top of my voice.

I bundled the two out of the room and banged the door shut. Undaunted, they went on banging at the door. I cared a hoot. Shakeela made an attempt to open the door. I challenged her.

"Why did you push the children out?" she barked.

"Do I need your permission to discipline my children?" I shot back, and gave her a push.

"Won't you stop hurling questions at each other and open the door?" our son screamed, attacking the door with a cricket bat.

"Have you both gone mad?" our daughter shouted, pounding the door with a pestle.

I refused to budge and pressed my back hard against the rattling door.

"Won't you stop battering the door?" Shakeela shouted back. "Don't you understand your father is raising hell over nothing to get a pretext for not taking us on the pilgrimage?"

"For heaven's sake, won't you please stop shooting questions?" our son shot back.

Before Shakeela could retort with a question, I heard Murari yell, "What the hell is going on here? Will you open the door or shall I have to break it open?"

Matters had spilled from our apartment. How bad! I stepped aside and Shakeela opened the door.

Our kindly neighbour was a born peacemaker. He was patient and persuasive. He heard all the four of us and came to the following conclusions.

One: I was losing the glamour that was mine as a suave

and composed gentleman and was getting increasingly irritable every new dawn.

Two: My bad temper was of the type that forced one's mate react by hurling questions that can only elicit questions as answer.

Three: Our children belonged to a very unfortunate lot who often got drowned in an eddy of questions and could only cry for help asking questions.

Four: All this was because there was a big question mark on the *vaastu* of our apartment.

"The builder trapped you into buying this apartment by offering a five-thousand-rupees discount," Murari told me. "No man who knows at least the general requirements of *vaastu* would buy this apartment."

"What is *vaastu*, brother?" Shakeela asked.

Murari's head shook in utter disappointment.

"How sad you do not even know the meaning of *vaastu*," he moaned. "That explains how alienated you are from our culture. *Vaastu* is to a dwelling place what horoscope is to an individual. You are in the midst of a double calamity. There is not only incompatibility among your horoscopes and those of your pets, as Sampat Iyer has testified, but there is also a horrendous distortion of *vaastu* principles in the layout of your apartment. This late-night attack at your door by your children is an indisputable indication that you are undergoing the direct consequences of the flawed *vaastu* of your dwelling. It's an emergency."

He rushed to our phone and dialled a number, a misdemeanour so uncharacteristic of him. On other days he would not even pick up and read our newspaper without asking permission. He called one Pandit Shingdi and asked him to rush immediately to our apartment. He insisted it was a late-night emergency that the pandit should not decline. There was a smile of satisfaction when he hung up. This brought Pandit Shingdi to our apartment in ten minutes.

Pandit Shingdi was a handsome man who would not have seen more than forty summers. He was dressed like a prince. The glitter of gold and precious stones attacked our eyes from every part of his body above the waist. His profession was no doubt earning him good money. The wry expression he put on as soon as entered our apartment confirmed our neighbour's opinion that our apartment was a hell by *vaastu* standards. Our neighbour briefed him on our troubles in such detail that it surprised me that a neighbour could be so informed about our lives, including our daily routine.

"*Vaastu* is a divine science," Pandit Shingdi spoke at last. "The trouble this household is facing should be an eye-opener to you about the perils one invites by looking down upon it." The pandit went on to give a long lecture on the eternal efficacy of *vaastu* in determining the wellbeing of people and nations, narrating umpteen examples drawn from his illustrious career. India, he said, is doomed forever because of its wrong *vaastu*. That the land should slope down to the northeast, should be highest at the southwest corner and waterways should flow to the northeast, are the fundamental requirements of vaastu. They are all just the reverse about India. India has the highest mountains to the north, low islands to its southwest and all except one of its main rivers, including its holiest and most important river, Ganges, flow to the southeast, the direction that stands for death and destruction. India will never come good in Kaliyuga and the Ganges is destined to carry corpses till it dries up like the mythical Saraswati.

The example clearly brought home to me the finality of vaastu dictates, although it was a shock to hear that my country was irrevocably doomed. There was but a positive side to it. I, for the first time, could appreciate our government which did not waste its time trying to lift this country from the bottom. The vaastu consultants must have advised them on the futility of such efforts. So, they wisely concentrated their energies in the more useful enterprise of amassing wealth and holding on to power. Sound judgement indeed!

Pandit Shingdi suggested many alterations to the layout of our apartment, which would set right its *vaastu* problems. It was a relief to know that our apartment was not a hopeless case like our country. As per the new layout, the kitchen and the master bedroom would swap positions, the hall's width would be almost halved to allow space for a passage through which we could enter the apartment from the northeast, and most our doors and windows would be relocated. We were given instructions about where we should place each of our furniture and in which direction we should lie down or sit.

"Please mark the exact position of our TV and the direction it should face for India to win every cricket match," our son requested.

Our daughter chuckled.

"It's no laughing matter," Pandit Shingdi admonished our daughter.

Our son felt vindicated, and he let it known by knuckling his sister on the head.

"*Vaastu* does play a critical role in the outcome of every match," Pandit Shingdi continued, undeterred. "We in the *Vaastu Saastra* Association of India are distressed, as is every citizen, over the continuous downslide of Indian cricket. The resilience that our people are exhibiting in mutely bearing up endless waves of miseries that lash our nation is directly proportionate to the popularity cricket has been gaining. The prediction is that the misery of our people, especially of the very poor, will greatly increase in the days to come. It's therefore important that continuous setbacks should not cause a downslide in cricket's popularity."

"You have a point there, *panditji*," I said.

"I'm glad you are getting the point," Pandit Shingdi continued. "Cricket has happily become a cheap and affordable intoxicant for keeping our impoverished masses on a high even when their stomachs are pinching-empty and their heads are swollen with unfulfilled hopes and yearnings. A bloody revolution is brewing in the country and is sure to take place if cricket is allowed to lose its hold on the national psyche. So we decided to conduct an in-depth study about the *vaastu* angle of the malaise afflicting the great game and prescribe a remedy. The study covered every aspect of the game and took one full year to complete. In the end, it was a rewarding effort, which conclusively proved that the *vaastu* of everything, from the stadium in which a match is played to the factory in which the balls, stumps, bats and pads are manufactured, from the players' dressing rooms to the hotels where the players and officials are put up, from the pitch to the direction in which the players' wives sit and watch the game, all have a definite bearing on the outcome of every match. We have submitted a detailed report on the findings to the Ministry of Sports."

"What's the response?" Shakeela asked.

"We are fortunate to have a Minister of Sports who shares our conviction that the inspiring science of *vaastu* can solve cricket's problems. The Minister has accepted all our recommendations and is earnestly executing them."

"Will India then win all the matches from now on?"

our son asked.

"Not every match. India will definitely win every home series. India will hardly win a match abroad, because the competing countries will do everything they can to thwart our *vaastu* requirements on their home grounds. But our minister has decided to tackle that problem by playing fewer matches abroad on patriotic grounds. So, thanks to *vaastu saastra*, we should end up winning a majority of the matches we play."

It was my prerogative as the man of the house to ask the last question.

"Is there really no remedy for the hopeless *vaastu* of our country?" I asked.

"We arrived at one during the last National Convention of *Vaastu* Pandits. We have proposed two major remedies to the government. One is to build a tower, a foot taller than Mount Everest on the southwestern-most island of Lashwadeep. It will make the southwestern point of our country the highest. The other is to dig a tunnel through the Himalayas and divert the Ganges to China so that it flows to the northeast. This would set right the *vaastu* of our country and make it prosperous."

"But are they feasible?"

"Why not? They're simpler than building nuclear bombs. Don't underestimate our technological calibre."

"Where will we get the colossal sum required?"

Shakeela asked.

"We might have to earmark the entire development fund in the budget for half a century to meet the expenses, but the nation will prosper forever after that. Won't it be better than continuing in this sorry state forever?" the pandit asked, his eyebrows rising to emphasize the question.

I had but to agree that it was a grand idea. I decided that very moment to vote for the party that would espouse the project during the ensuing elections.

When Pandit Shingdi took leave of us, my hope of getting done the alterations he had suggested for our apartment had receded by three thousand rupees. In fact, I did not have the money to start the work at all, and I told Murari as much. The kindly neighbour came to my rescue again. He convinced the other apartment owners that it was also to their interest that our apartment got remodelled to suit *vaastu*. All of them contributed generously and thus ensured that the entire complex in which our apartment was situated was quarantined from the bad effects of flawed *vaastu*. We were even left with sufficient surplus for our countrywide pilgrimage.

It looked as though I had not clearly understood every detail of the instructions Pandit Shingdi had given, because our household continued to be haunted by the old problems. We actually became more hostile towards each other. Our son got into demoniac fits each time India lost a cricket match. (India lost all but one out of the eight matches of the home series that was about to conclude.) It was in such a gloomy mood that my children and I gathered around our TV, facing towards the northeast, and watched the last match of the series. It was a day-night match. A short shower had delayed the match by an hour. The last ball was being bowled at ten to midnight. India's Arjun was the bowler. If the Pakistani batsman would hit the ball for a four, India's bitter opponents would win the match. It was heart-stopping suspense. The bowler was taking an excruciatingly long time to rub his balls and polish his ass with the red ball before he sends it down to create history. Fingernails were getting chewed up fast. As the bowler approached the crease, tension got the upper hand of our daughter and she drew her chair close to the TV, drastically changing its direction. Arjun's ball was hit for a mighty six in the southwest direction and India lost the match.

"We lost the match because of you," my son screamed at his sister. "Why did you shift your chair?"

"Who are you to question me?" my daughter hit back. "Do I need your permission to shift my chair?"

"How dare you challenge me after making India lose?"

"How the hell am I responsible for Arjun sending down a sitter?"

"Didn't Pandit Shingdi warn India is sure to lose a match

if we watch it sitting in that direction?"

"Now, why are you both fighting just because India lost a match?" I intervened.

"How could she betray our country like this, papa?" my son burst out sobbing, his right hand stretched out accusingly at his sister. "How could she be so unpatriotic?"

"Papa, will you ask him to apologise for accusing me of betraying my country or will I have to punch him in his tummy and force him to do it?" my daughter threatened, quaking.

"Now, what's this?" I intervened again. "Are you going to tear at each other just because India lost a cricket match?"

"How can we bear India losing to Pakistan, papa? And why don't you feel guilty that your daughter has caused it all by shifting her chair to the wrong direction?" There was less of anger and more of agony in my son's voice.

Shakeela came rushing from the bedroom and frowned at me.

"Didn't I ask you to switch off the TV at ten and come to bed?" she yelled. "What more did you think you could achieve by sitting awake and watching a silly game than spoiling my mood and setting the children at each other?"

"How dare you call cricket silly?" our son roared, and rushed at his mother. He punched her repeatedly on her buttocks.

I rushed to Shakeela's rescue.

Matters went out of control and came to such a pass that we shot questions indiscriminately at each other until we had pushed each other to the road and started shooting questions at passers-by. We returned to our apartment after midnight when we could get none to shoot questions at. The doors of our apartment were wide open when we returned. I remembered we had left them so.

Tragedy had befallen our house while we were away out on the road. Our cat and parakeet lay dead. They were so dear to us. Our children were inconsolable for the whole of the night and for many more days and nights.

Pussy cat, my pussy cat,
How soft the touch of your paws!
Sorry for the times I beat you

When you scratched with your claws.
Pussy cat, my pussy cat,
How bright they, your marble eyes!
Swished they through the darkness thick,

Like the flashing shooting stars.
Pussy cat, my pussy cat,
How warm the feel of your fur!
As you cuddled close to me,
While I floated on blithe dreams.
Parakeet, my parakeet,
How melodious your song!

Sorry for the times I teased you
Till I made you shed tears.
Parakeet, my parakeet,
How red your short shapely beak!

Many an hour did I spent,
Watching you peck grains in glee.
Parakeet, my parakeet,
How rich in shades they, your plumes!

God almighty made the hues
Seeing you fly in the sky.

It was the first time that a real tragedy had befallen us; it was the first time we suffered the great pain of loss. In the grief, we forgot about fighting over trifles. Peace returned to our home.

After a few days, Murari consoled us saying, "Sampat Iyer was right, the horoscopes of your cat and parakeet were the real problem."

A week later, a top cricketer spilt the beans, telling a shocked nation that every cricket match India played was fixed.

Chapter - 3

The Party

A few months into the mysterious death of our pets and the descent of heavenly peace into our home, I noticed a sudden spurt in the fortune of our neighbour, Murari. He began to flaunt a lifestyle that mocked the salary he earned. I would often wonder at his skill in squeezing the lifestyle of a large family of wife and eight children to the limits of the salary he earned as an Assistant Curator of the city's zoo. He even pinched money by himself dressing his children's hair. He had always bestowed on me the deference and awe that was, by tradition, a comparatively affluent neighbour's right. Such a man was now taunting me by stacking his apartment with every imaginable type of luxury appliance and electronic gadget. He even bought a new car!

The glare of his Rolex watch and golden spectacles blinded me and the whir of his car shook my ego more often than I could stand. He overtook me by leaps and bounds, becoming worthy of the deference and awe he once had for me, which I was determined not to give. His prosperity shattered my ego and my inside began to fret and fume at the very sight of him. I began to imagine every kind of diabolic reason for his suddenly getting so rich. I finally put the seal of affirmation to my suspicion that he had killed our pets. Still, I was willing to concede that he had charitable intentions when he strangled the sweet things. He did it for our good. But I began to assume that, that act of charity had opened the floodgates of fortune for him.

I was, by now, fairly aware of the oddities that could influence human life. Experience had taught me that a cruel act could also bring good luck. I myself had real experiences of the inauspicious becoming the auspicious. Here is one such case.

I lost favour with my father as a natural consequence of marrying a woman addicted to the veil. (It must be said to his credit that he overlooked the fact that she had earlier lived a couple of months with a sheikh, because he strongly believed that intimacy with royal blood could ennoble a commoner.) He gave me only half-an-acre out of the seven acres that I would have got if I had not lowered my repute before him. Had not my brothers refused to take the half-acre plot, because it had a defunct anthill which a cobra had made its home, where none would dare to cultivate, live in or even defecate on such a land, he would not have given me even that. That patrimony only served the purpose of continuously reminding me that my father not only disowned me but also hated me more than anything else in the world. I bore up the insult in gratitude for the love my father had lavished on me till the fortunate day I married my wonderful wife.

I abandoned the plot of land to the cobra.

One day, I got a letter from a man who wrote that he wanted to buy the plot and begged in a two-page entreaty that I should not refuse him. He offered a substantial premium on the market price and added that he was ready with the amount and I could effect the sale any time. I found the letter's content hard to believe and suspected some treachery. I imagined that my father and brothers were luring me to my native village to remove the blotch that I was to the pre-eminent Hindu clan of Ulakam.

I made discreet enquiries. I had the greatest surprise yet of my life when I learned that the man who wrote to me was a genuine buyer. He was an unfortunate man slipping down the ladder of life every passing moment for no other reason than that he was born under a peculiar star which would beam fortune on him only if he lived in a plot that a cobra had made its abode. I sold the land to him and lit my house with the dazzle of money.

So why could I not conclude that killing our pets had brought luck to our neighbour? Now, tell me, how a man, who would himself dress his children's hair to make both ends meet, could afford things that even the rich bought only in instalments. (I was not willing to buy the argument that the rich were circumventing Income Tax rules by opting to hire-purchase.) I was as certain as my star would permit that my neighbour had unlocked the treasure trove of first-degree fortune by killing our pets. If you have a heart, you will now appreciate why mine bled when he flaunted his fortune.

At first, I resolved to handle the threat he posed to my ego by buying a better brand of every home luxury bought. The money my patrimony unexpectedly brought came in handy for it. But I had to fear Shakeela. She detested luxuries even more than I detested Murari's new status. It was as if she had a phobia for gadgets that made life more comfortable. When I offered to buy an electric grinder, she objected saying she would bloat and look ugly if she stopped grinding by hand. When I offered to buy a refrigerator, she asked why should we use frozen meat and fish when fresh meat and fish were available aplenty. When I offered to buy an air conditioner, she objected saying we would become cold people. I had to get her around to accepting these things before I brought them home. But that was more easily said than done. Finally, I thought a way out.

I celebrated my wife's thirtieth birthday on a grand scale. I invited all my friends and all the inmates of our residential complex for the party. I bought the home appliances I wanted and asked a few of my close friends to present them to Shakeela at the party. In fact, my friends were as zealous as I to break Shakeela's obscurantist abhorrence of modern comforts (many of them had stopped paying us visits because they wouldn't get even a tumbler of cold water to drink when they visited us.)

The idea worked. Shakeela was so overwhelmed by the affection my friends showed that she gladly accepted all the gifts they offered. It didn't matter that she seldom used them. I had my purpose served.

But Murari wouldn't allow my soul to enjoy the peace for very long. He forced my envy out into the open when he decided to celebrate the silver jubilee of his wedding. He was only forty-five though he wished to celebrate it in a style that would win him admission into the exclusive club of the parvenu, the category that was the envy of the city and torment of its decadent aristocracy. When he came to invite us for the function, he took me into confidence about every detail of the grandiose scale of it, including the price of the dress and jewellery he and his wife would wear on the occasion, something that would involve a mind-boggling amount. His wife would wear a sari that would cost a hundred thousand! It was uncharitable of him to have told me the details in advance. Why didn't he have thought for the pain I would suffer listening to the list of things we couldn't even dream of? I had no doubt he did it purposely to give me sleepless nights. I decided to pay him back in his own coin.

I looked out for a car, a richer one than Murari's, which I could get on hire for a few months. An office colleague introduced me to a man who was in desperate straits for money and was willing to sell his car at half the price at which he had bought it a few months ago. It seemed as though even God was sympathizing with me. I bought the car and drove it home seven days before Murari's wedding anniversary. I parked it next to his car. The next morning I walked to my car as my neighbour was unlocking the door of his with a key. I stood at a distance, took out a remote from my pocket and pressed on it. I then slipped into my car before he could unlock his. Murari gaped at my car in dismay.

Getting classy dress and jewellery fo Shakeela that would beat those of Mrs. Murari was far more difficult. My money had got practically exhausted. I searched for some agency from which I could hire them. I could find none. Finally, as luck would have it, I discovered an impoverished heroin-hooked prince four days before the anniversary party. His royal depravities had driven his young wife to suicide and he managed to sustain himself in the clouds by renting out the rare jewellery and dress of his wife. I got the dress dry-cleaned and the jewellery burnished to make them look new. They weren't really very old and the vamping up gave them an overpowering glitter. Shakeela tried the dress on and she agreed to take it too in her stride after she had had a look at herself in the mirror. She looked no less charming than the legendary Noorjahan.

"The dress is a great piece. How much did it cost?" she asked.

"I hired it for today's party."

"For how much?"

"Two thousand."

"And the car?"

"I bought it for two hundred thousand."

"Our neighbour's wedding anniversary is costing us a fortune. Does neighbourly love demand so much?" I felt happy I had succeeded in hiding my jealous intentions from her.

"We should celebrate and rejoice more than them for what they have achieved," I said. "That's true neighbourly love. Monetary considerations should not smother such noble sentiments. Living together for twenty-five years and prospering greatly in the process is a tough proposition these days. I am spending money to let them know that we acknowledge them as great people who made it against all odds, and also not to be an embarrassment to them when they introduce us to their affluent guests as their immediate neighbours."

"I'm afraid you are taking upon yourself too great a financial risk for putting noble thoughts into practice."

"God will bless us for it by giving us the joy of living together for at least fifty years."

"God should... when your intentions are right."

My mired mind made me think for a moment that she was having a dig at me. But the doubt cleared when she asked me to take her to a beauty parlour.

The wedding anniversary fell on a Saturday. There was a dispute about it though. There were two opinions about on which day and at what moment the Muraris would enter the twenty-sixth year of their married life. Sampat Iyer drove a spike into the commonsense view that a wedding anniversary falls on the date of marriage as per the Gregorian calendar and stirred up a hornet's nest. He argued that the anniversary would fall only on the day when the stars of the Muraris would fall into the same ideal combination (in the endearing posture, as a mischievous astrologer once suggested) as at the *muhurat* when they were married. Murari's father-in-law, himself an astrologer of merit, joined issue with Sampat Iyer arguing that if that were the case, the *muhurat* of the first night, the auspicious day of consummation of the marriage which had occurred ten days after the wedding day, should have had the final say in deciding on which day the anniversary would fall. It was the day when Ganesh Murari and Savita Bhat melted in the heat of love and began the process of producing future generations of Muraris. The dispute flared into such a crisis that it occasioned the conclave of twenty-five renowned astrologers (one for each year of the Muraris' wedded life) who discussed the matter threadbare for three days and finally came to the consensus that the jubilee would be hosted on the day when the *muhurat* of their wedding reoccurred and they would sleep together again only when the *muhurat* of their first night reoccurred, which would be two hundred and twenty-six days later, the long gap between the *muhurat*s correctly mirroring the hiatus between marriage and nuptial bliss that the passage of time had brought about. The stars do not miss any detail!

The Muraris were to start from home for the function hall at three forty-five in the afternoon, fifteen minutes before the inauspicious period of *rahu* would commence. I had decided that I would sabotage the wedding anniversary party. How in the world could I accept Muraris becoming the newest addition to the city's high society? I would by no means allow them to acquire a status that was not first mine. I wouldn't mind selling my soul to Lucifer to achieve the purpose.

Lucifer came to my help even before I approached him and whispered into my ears, "Deflate the tires of Murari's car." The work was so simple that I saluted the fallen angel and sneaked into the basement where the car was parked, just before the Muraris were to start, and flattened the tires by pricking the valves with a toothpick.

When the deflated tires made the Muraris sweat in their blatant party dress, I played the goodly neighbour and offered them a lift. They accepted the offer and had just got into my car when Murari's father-in-law intervened.

"Wait a minute, children." he said, "Let's check the numerological suitability of this car's number."

The old man strained his numerological wisdom for a few excruciating minutes before he authoritatively ruled that my car's number did not make good bedfellow with the birth dates of either of the Muraris and so he would by no means allow his children to travel by it and put their lives in peril. The ruling created a first rate crisis, because, by the time it was pronounced, inauspicious *rahu* had set in. *Rahu* would prevail for one and half hours more and the Muraris would not be able to move an inch forward all that while. The immediate fallout was that the party would get inordinately delayed. More importantly, the wedding anniversary *muhurat* would be missed, with dire consequences for the Muraris. They were doomed!

The elite of the city were waiting for the Muraris at the banquet hall of Hotel Skyrocket International. *Rahu* could be no excuse for making them wait for over one and a half hours. Neither could they, for any reason whatsoever, jeopardise their future as husband and wife by venturing out while *rahu* was on. I got out of the car. They sat inside, fretting and sweating.

The tires of Murari's car could easily have been made robust during the long wait, but Murari concurred with his father-in-law that using the ill-fated car could spell disaster. Besides, the Muraris could not come out of my car, because that would amount to taking a step backward, which was as ominous as setting out during *rahu*. So they continued to sit inside, watching the hands of their watches move forward laboriously. The numerological problem of my car was solved by replacing the number plate of my car with that of Murari's car – a wrong done for a good cause.

"Will the guests wait much longer?" Murari asked me. "Won't they go away?"

"Looks like they will find it the most sensible thing to do," I replied.

"The party will then have ended before it started. I must save the party. Please suggest some way out."

Here was a chance to hide my role in creating the crisis.

"I have an idea," I said after a pause. "Someone could explain the situation to the guests and then get the drinks and floorshow started. That will hold the guests back and keep them in good spirits."

"That's a great idea. Would you mind catching a taxi and going to the hotel? No one can manage the show at the hotel better than you. My chauffeur will drive your car for us."

I was hesitant. The idea didn't at all sound good to me. It would defeat the very purpose for which I had bought my car. Murari would travel like a prince in my car.

"That's the best thing to do," Shakeela said. "Come, let's go." She rushed out of the basement.

What else could I do than follow her? She hailed a cab. I followed her into it. "Skyrocket," she told the driver. "We are in a hurry."

We sped to the hotel.

"Who do you think must have deflated the tires?" Shakeela asked, as we were nearing the hotel.

"Some mischievous kid, who else?"

"I don't think so. Some envious man must have done it."

"You're reading too much into it. The Muraris are such good people; I can't imagine anyone acting so malevolently towards them."

"A lot of people have been gritting with envy because of the good fortune that has come their way. One of them must have done it to sabotage the party."

Was Shakeela's nose capable of smelling wily schemes too?

"Don't unnecessarily make uncharitable guesses. It's just a prank played by some kid."

"Murari's chauffeur said he had inspected the car just ten minutes earlier. The tyres were okay then. I saw you go into the basement a little after he came out. Did you see anyone loiter in the basement?"

"No, I did not see anyone."

Shakeela turned towards me. I knew she had turned to cast a suspicious look. Her keen nose was playing havoc again. I had to somehow convince her that her nose was misleading her if our marriage was to last till our wedding silver jubilee.

"Maybe his chauffeur has done it?" I reasoned. "He must be harbouring some deep grudge against the Muraris. He often grumbles to me that he has to slog eighteen hours a day and doesn't get paid anything for the extra hours of work he puts in."

"The man is in greater agony than the Muraris because of what happened. He was weeping inconsolably."

"He must be pretending."

"It's not that difficult to make out who is pretending and who is not."

We were already at the entrance of Hotel Skyrocket International. I got as flattened as the deflated tires of Murari's car and was left with no more strength than needed to curse Shakeela's malicious nose.

I still had one more chance to impress upon Shakeela that her nose was wrong. I decided that I would manage the show at the banquet hall with such zeal to save the situation for Murari that she would rue her suspicion about my role in the mush that the Muraris found themselves in, which I suspected she was hinting at.

"Ladies and gentlemen!" I addressed the guests from the podium of the banquet hall, "Unforeseeable circumstances have forced a slight alteration in our programme. Some malicious urchin deflated the tires of the car that was to bring the jubilarians to this hall. By the time an alternative could be arranged, *rahu* had set in. As you will well appreciate, they cannot set out till *rahu* has passed. It's obvious that this elite gathering cannot be made to wait till then. We shall have a jolly good time as we wait for them. It's my pleasure to announce on behalf of the Muraris the commencement of the floorshow and drinks."

"Hurray!" the hall reverberated.

The hearty response gave me great impetus. Armed with a winning smile and a sweet tongue, I mesmerised the guests and made them almost forget that they had gathered to celebrate the sliver wedding anniversary of the Muraris, and endeared myself to all. It was a picturesque crowd.

There were great celebrities
Of friendly disposition,
Which neatly hid their frailties
Or bitter composition.

There were intelligent men
Who got drowned in discussion
About films, cricket 'n women,
Their brains' supreme obsession.

There were men who with shrewd tricks
Sold governmental projects,
Far from the gaze of critics
To whose jeer they were objects.

There was a lover of art
Whose dimples and broad sweet smile,
Majestic gait and looks smart
Sent love waves for a long mile.

There was a funny short guy
With quite serious looks;
His jokes bid sorrows good-bye
And fought the malice of crooks.

A woman gifting sad smiles
Persued a youth of gay frown.
They beat each other in styles
With freaky pants and guilt gown.

A poet with a goatee
Sang throttled thoughts in verses
In voice that was so hearty,
But suffered sad reverses.

Shakeela was so eye-filling in her royal dress that men whirled around her like honeybees. The Prince of Sopar, who had rented out her dress, was also among the guests. It appeared as though it was the first full opportunity he got to leisurely admire his wife's dress. He was mostly hovering around Shakeela, with a goblet in hand. I liked the way Shakeela stood embarrassedly. Never before did she look so comely, in any other mood or at any other occasion. I disturbed the men and the mood only once, when I went close and whispered to her, "What difference would it make even if the crisis were caused by the treachery of an envious soul? See how cheerful the guests are. I'm so happy the crisis has blown over for the Muraris."

Deep within me, I was expecting the guests would start sneering down their host once the drink got into their heads. That's how it was in every party I had the fortune of attending. I imagined they would say:

'See the fun of it, a party made to stand on its head because of *rahu*!'

'Do you know which the greatest wonder of the modern world is? It's this 'hostless' party.'

'Money can't fetch culture.'

'I can take up the task of civilising them if they will pay a fat fee.'

'How on earth did Murari get so rich so suddenly?'

'He is a first rate international smuggler. There is no other way an Assistant Curator of a zoo could amass so much wealth in no time.'

'The birds in his zoo must be laying golden eggs.'

'He must have got the riches by selling his soul to the devil.'

Instead, one of them got on to the podium and sang paeans to the Muraris. "I congratulate the Muraris," he said, "for their courageous decision not to violate *rahu*. In the normal course, this party would have been a fiasco. Because they chose to abide by *rahu*, which is going to delay their arrival here for about two hours, all of us might have gone home. We would have scorned them and ostracised them. They risked all that to uphold the sanctity of *rahu* in these times when it is a fashion to ridicule such divine disciplines. They also did a service by giving us a chance to collectively proclaim our adherence to *rahu* by enjoying this gala party in their absence." He raised his half-filled goblet. "Cheers to the Muraris!"

"Cheers!" all the throats burst out in unison.

That was unbearable. I couldn't stand watching my brainwork being made Murari's victory stand. I had to do something to reverse the mood of the guests subtly and set it against Murari. I had played a good host on behalf of Murari till then and had not taken any drink. I needed some good amount of it now to make my brain throw up some devilish idea. I had three quick drinks. I danced to the jumpy tune the orchestra was playing, thinking. I stopped when I got a bright flash.

I went to the man who had turned Murari into a hero with his devotion to *rahu*. "I must thank you, sir," I told him, "for your magnanimous words that cleared all fears of the displeasure the guest might have had because of the complications *rahu* had created. Please repeat to the Muraris what you said when they come. They are very upset. Your words will comfort them greatly. There is just one more glitch; the *muhurat* for the exchange of garlands has passed." The exchange of garlands had just recently been made the crowning part of the official religious ceremony for wedding anniversary celebrations, which itself was a recent adaptation of a Western institution.

"If the *Muhurat* has passed, there can be no exchange of garlands," the champion of *rahu* proclaimed.

"But won't the function be meaningless without it?" I asked.

"If the *muhurat* has passed, there can be no exchange of garlands, and if there'll be no exchange of garlands, there'll be no meaningful anniversary celebration. There can be no two opinions about that. This'll then be no more than a jolly get-together."

"Will they have a second chance to celebrate the jubilee?"

"No, they won't. There can be only one *muhurat* for a function. If they have missed it, it is their *karma*. It could be the result of some grave sin they or their forefathers have committed. Whatever be the case, they just have got to accept it."

"Isn't that too cruel? I beg you please cooperate to have the exchange of garlands gone through."

"I'm not going to cooperate, and take it from me I'll do my best to see that few others will also do the same. *Muhurat*s maintain the harmony of the universe. If they are violated, everything will go haywire. Horses could grow horns, pigs could have chicken-heads, men could have boobs, the sun could rise in the west, asses could start talking, men could start braying, and what not."

I was happy things were again squaring up. The wedding party would, after all, end up an utter flop.

The Muraris arrived at last. The drunken guests welcomed them with a raucous swell of cheers. A smile blossomed on their faces. The poet with a goatee got on to the podium and sang:

Hark! Ye hark! I'll sing a song of love;
Sang a smart young boy once the first note,
From below his lover's balcony,
Mantra of love's first ceremony.

Hark! Ye hark! I'll sing a song of love,
Sang a sweet young girl then the next note,
Showering hot kisses on her beau,
As he bent in love's pain like a bow.

Hark! Ye hark! I'll sing a song of love,
A devout old priest sang the next note,
Joining two souls in eternal bond,
Blessed them to sink in love's depthless pond.

Hark! Ye hark! I'll sing a song of love,
Woman in birth pains sang the fourth note,
Torn apart to bring forth to the world,
Love's fruit from where it formed, lying curled.

Hark! Ye hark! I'll sing a song of love,
Man in boundless joy sang the fifth note,

Holding in arms his babe who would bleep,
Until it was lullabied to sleep.

Hark! Ye hark! I'll sing a song of love,
Two inseparables sang the sixth note,
Living twenty-five long years as one.
Heroes they who love's most battles won.

Hark! Ye hark! I'll sing a song of love,
The last note is left yet to be sung.
After eons seven may it from
Angels' bugles up in heaven come.

The poet got a standing ovation, and that made the head *pujari* impatient to start his performance. He walked to the *pooja mandapam*, trailed by his assistants and the Muraris. A wave of conspiratorial rumours ruffled the hall. The champion of *rahu* and *muhurat* tromped towards the door to march out. The guests turned and followed him enbloc like a herd. I imagined that the door would open and, in minutes, the banquet hall would empty out and I would have vanquished Murari! My eyes closed tight in unbearable joy.

Oh, gosh! A divine guest flung the doors open from outside. I opened my eyes and saw His Holiness Satsang Baba standing at the door, holding back the herd with his hands raised in blessing. The Muraris rushed to the godman's feet. He placed his hands on their heads and declared, "These are my devotees in whom I am well pleased. I have come now to redeem them from a disaster. The powers of evil have conspired to deprive them of the muhurat on this momentous occasion. Accursed are they! I have come to spoil their evil designs. I am the beginning and the end. Time will flee, but not from me. The muhurat is here. I am the muhurat. Let the pooja start!"

The banquet hall turned full throat, 'Om Baba, Satsang Baba', 'Om Baba, Satsang Baba.'

The chant shook the hotel. Alarmed, its other occupants ran down and rushed out. But the chant continued in full force till the pooja got over and the Muraris exchanged garlands. I locked myself up in a toilet and wept.

I heard a shriek of terror. It was Shakeela screaming for help! I stormed back into the banquet hall. Shakeela was thrashing about like a child to get out of the grip of the Prince of Sopar who was all over her. "Leave her!" I yelled, and pummelled the assaulter with my fists.

"I'll not leave her; she is my beloved," the prince crooned, pressing Shakeela tighter.

The guests stood aghast and watched. Satsang Baba stood unconcerned. Desperate, I bit the prince on his ass. He writhed and let go of Shakeela, lying flat on his back and osculating the air. I ran out with Shakeela, snatched my keys from Murari's chauffeur, and drove home. Shakeela lay in the backseat, crying. I dared not utter a word.

Back at home, Shakeela went straight into our room and rummaged the wardrobe. I got into terrible fears. She took out the veil! She was putting it on!

"Please, no!" I cried. "Don't put that veil on again!"

She held the veil aloft, glared at me like Durga, and blasted, "The veil was a part of me from the age of thirteen. I discarded it and changed my identity to please you, because you gave me an identity after a venerator of the veil discarded me after using me. You were so noble a soul until envy took possession of you. It has distorted you and turned you into a devil. I followed every despicable thing envy made you do. I did not see you go to the basement, but I could judge that it was you who deflated the tires. You are a great schemer, but your eyes reveal everything. I could read your guilt in them. How could you sink so low? Your nobility made me discard this veil and don the princess' dress. Years ago, you saw my naked face and saved me from insignificance. Because of you, today I suffered the desecration I feared then. I'll put on the veil and become my old self again. My old self is what you deserve now."

She put the black veil on. As it slid down to cover her all over, its darkness enveloped and froze me.

Someone rang the doorbell. Neither of us moved. The bell rang again, now for quite a longer while. I stood frozen.

Shakeela went to see who it was.

The late-night visitors were two policemen and the man who had sold me my car. The car was a stolen one. The man who sold it to me at a dirt-cheap price was a professional vehicle lifter. The thief's confession implicated me in collaborating with him in stealing the car. I was paying a heavy price for my envy. I offered to surrender my car and forego the money I paid for it. But that alone would not do. The police demanded a huge price for squashing the case and pushing it under the carpet. I pleaded I did not have the money they demanded. Finally, they agreed to be contented with the money and jewellery I had.

The thief phoned me up the next morning.

"The case can't be hushed up unless I too cooperate," he said.

"What do you mean?"

"I mean I don't mind making an open confession that you bought my service to steal the car. I know I'll have to go to jail along with you if I do so, but jail is sweet home for me."

"Are you trying to blackmail me?"

"No, not that. It just happens that I need some money urgently. It was only natural that I immediately thought of an old acquaintance like you."

"For what should I pay you money? For cheating me? You won't get a paisa, you son of a bitch!"

"Now, don't use vulgar language, because that could raise my demand very high. I know you have little money or jewellery left with you. Don't get frustrated. It would suffice if you gave me your TV, fridge, air conditioners and things like that. Only, the list is quite exhaustive, because I'll have to sell them at less than half their price."

Whatever the cost, I wouldn't allow myself to be branded a thief. I had to give in to his demand.

The thief came and took away every luxury item I had bought to get one up on Murari, and more.

And for me was left only a vengeful soul and the haunting blackness of the veil.

Chapter - 4

The Hidden Treasure

Had not Shakeela slighted me by getting back into the veil, I would have pleaded guilty and begged pardon of her. I felt miserable for what had happened to her at the banquet hall. It was all my fault. My envy had caused it. But now, made a villain, my overpowering feeling was one of vengeance. I had descended very low from the decent gentleman I once was. I would plunge deeper if needed to pull down Murari and tear Shakeela's veil into shreds.

I decided I would handle the veil first. I would not have recourse to physical violence, because I was a victim of the superstitious belief that no man of worth should subdue his wife with muscle power. Besides, why was there the need of it when I could use my son to get the work done? The children were not shocked to see their mother hiding herself behind a black veil. But they found it a little strange when Shakeela started putting on the veil whenever anyone other than a close kin visited us – she did it purposely to spite me. They got used to that too very soon. My only chance lay in linking the destruction of the veil to some big request my son would make. The opportunity came only too soon.

The Indian government lifted the ban on cricket matches with Pakistan, which had come into force from the day the top man of that country called the top man our country 'a Kashmiri goat'. The recall of the ban was made possible by a clarification from the top man of Pakistan after a ten-year gap that he had made a slip of the tongue and that he had actually intended to call his Indian counterpart 'a Himalayan goat'. The announcement of the repeal of the ban came in a late-night news bulletin. It was as if the two nations were rising to a new era of liberty, a new era of hope. Every city and village celebrated the announcement the whole night, dancing in the streets and bursting crackers. The frenzy loaded my son with the kind of zeal that would last a lifetime. The Board of Control for Cricket in India announced in the following week that the first test match between India and Pakistan after a decade would be played in our city.

"You must take me to the test, papa," my son demanded when he got me all alone – he knew Shakeela would shout him down if she heard him.

"I shall if you do me a favour in return," I replied, broke though I was.

"I shall do anything you ask. I shall even give my life for you after the test match is over."

"I want a much simpler favour, son."

"What's it, papa?"

I first gave him a lecture on the darkness that the black veil represented in our lives, repeating the same arguments that I had once used with Shakeela. My son listened seriously, giving me the impression that he was grasping the sad social, philosophical and religious implications of a veil, especially a black one. He asked me a week's time for tearing his mother's veil to bits.

For some months my son had been breathing fresh air and that, apparently, had the wholesome effect of making him look fairer and more relaxed. The announcement of the new test series between India and Pakistan polluted the air he breathed with so much cricket that, within twenty-four hours of our pact, he turned purple and aggressive. The usual repercussion followed. He took up his cricket bat and swung it in every direction, hitting the air for square cuts, off drives and hooks, mostly for fours and sixes. When he hit a huge six that would complete his sixth double century of the day, but this time the bat slipped out of his hand and unseated two glass tumblers from the dining table on to the floor. Shakeela glowered and snarled at him so viciously that whenever I recall it I wish I hadn't been there to witness her fury. The boy got scared for his life and screamed, "Why don't you wear the veil at home also and cover those vicious eyes?"

I could well understand the frightened child's reaction, but what a reversal it was! I waited with bated breath to see if Shakeela would rush for the veil. Fortunately, she did not. I fell back on my son's uncompromising devotion for cricket to reassure myself that he would keep his word. Shakeela's fiery eyes would not scorch his desire to watch the test match; he would suffer the heat of hell for it. Here was a rare occasion for cricket to make a positive contribution by aiding a noble cause, the disappearance of the veil from the face of the earth. The moment my son would tear Shakeela's veil into bits, I would inform cricket commentators the world over about the development. They would, at last, have something other than insufferable clichés like 'the glorious game of cricket' and 'the glorious game of uncertainties' to offer their listeners.

My son continued to score a dozen double centuries on average every day, though no more at the expense of glass tumblers (I took care that glass tumblers were nowhere in the vicinity of his bat when he hit his fours and sixes.) One more accident involving the bat and Shakeela would start wearing the veil at home too.

A week passed, but Shakeela's veil remained intact. My son insisted that I should buy the tickets for the test match first. He told me to my face that he did not trust I would keep my part of the pact once my work was done. He reminded me how I had once gone back on my word to buy him an elephant. That was when he was three years old. I had been urging him to do a somersault. He asked me what reward I would give him if he achieved the feat. I promised him an elephant. I wriggled out of my promise when he executed the somersault by presenting him an elephant shaped candy. How was I to know a three-year-old would remember it all his life and use it against me on occasions like this? I was cornered into buying the tickets in advance although I was convinced that it was a travesty of the spirit of our contract. I went with him to buy the tickets.

"Shall I buy the first day's or the last day's ticket?" I asked, standing in the queue at the counter.

"For all the five days of the test; that's our understanding."

"I never said so."

"You promised you would show me the test match. The match lasts five days."

"I don't have the money, son."

"How can you go back on your word and expect me to keep mine, papa?"

I understood the import of the tone of his question: No father can expect of his son the integrity he himself doesn't have – a very old truth that. It was no small tragedy that an attempt to save a few hundred rupees should have given my son a chance to pose so weighty a question to me. Shakeela's veil was landing me in too many humiliating situations. I was determined to brave them all with a visionary's zeal. I had a mission in life – to demolish the adamant veil. I gave in again to my son's blackmail and bought tickets for all the five days of the cricket test, after taking a promise from him that he would tear the veil before sunset the next day.

'WE WILL NOT ALLOW AN INDIA-PAK MATCH IN THE CITY', next morning's papers quoted Ravan. Ravan, president of the Patriotic Indians Party, whose goondas decided what should happen or not happen in our city, had the reputation of standing by his threats – my son was as aware of it as much as I was. He used Ravan's threat to suspend the destruction of the veil till the evening of the first day of the test match.

Ravan's patriotic hooligans stormed the stadium early in the morning of the first day of the match and dug up the pitch. The test match was cancelled and Shakeela's veil outlived the most serious threat it had yet faced. My son preserved the tickets as trophy of a desire unfulfilled.

While I lay floored by the veil, Murari was prospering by geometric progression. He got a promotion and became the curator of the city's zoo. He bought prime properties, took over a big textile unit, and launched a vernacular daily in a big way. At the home front, he did all that was needed to transform his wife from a hardworking housewife into an indolent *sethani*. There were two servants besides a cook to assist her. She bloated by the minute and when, within months, her girth increased beyond the reach of Murari's hands, he brought a slimming machine home and appointed a yoga instructor to bring her back into graspable size and pleasing shape. In contrast, Shakeela was reduced to a raw-boned miserable by backbreaking house chores and the added burden of the veil (I loved her enough to feel pity for her despite the veil).

Why was everything going so sour for me? Was the solar eclipse still haunting me with its dark effects? Or was I suffering the consequences of hurting my parents by marrying a woman-in-veil? Perhaps, they were all far-fetched fears of a depressed mind... But why was I searching for what I had guessed long ago? Wasn't the reversal of fortunes caused by the death of our pets? And why was I getting frustrated when there was a simple solution at hand? I would buy a cat and a parakeet as soon as I got my next pay and things would be rosy for me once again, and Murari's downfall would begin. But I had to take care that the horoscope of the new pets tallied with mine and not with Murari's, or else matters would get worse.

Pets with meticulously recorded horoscopes were now available in the market. The new business was the brainchild of the Prime Minister, who invented it to generate the ten million jobs he had promised on taking over the reins four years ago. The government gave an interest free loan of fifty thousand rupees and a subsidy of twenty-five thousand rupees to any postgraduate who was willing to rear and sell pets whose time of birth was correctly recorded and whose horoscopes were prepared by graduates who had passed out of the Astrology Faculty that the government had newly introduced at the universities. One million postgraduates were already employed in the business and the rest were waiting for new parakeets and lovebirds to get hatched. When the idea hit me, horoscope-recorded cats were easily available, but parakeets were in short supply. I was too impatient to wait till new parakeets got hatched. I paid a premium for the parakeet and brought the pets home after getting the compatibility of their stars with mine cross-checked by Sampat Iyer.

It worked! Mrs Murari started complaining to Shakeela that life was getting very boring and disgusting for her. Murari was seldom available at home. His official duty and his sprawling business kept him fully busy the whole day and he spent half the night in Satsang Baba's ashram. He came home exhausted after midnight, slumped into bed, and promptly sank into deep sleep.

Soon, I sort of started feeling better when Murari got richer and richer: The richer he got the more he spent his nights away from home. Discreet enquiries elicited from his chauffeur the information that he had of late started spending more nights at Satsang Baba's ashram than at home. It soon happened that he did not come home for weeks together. Things were definitely getting bad for the Muraris, at least in conjugal matters. It brought me not a little joy to see a morose Mrs Murari pass by my door.

One afternoon, Mrs. Murari walked in through my door while I was alone at home.

"Shakeela has gone away to her parents with the children for a couple of days," I said.

"She told me this morning she was going," Mrs Murari responded. "I came to talk to you all alone."

"My pleasure." I motioned her to the chair opposite me. "Please be seated."

"There was a time when we lived as very good neighbours. We were then concerned about each other. We always enquired about each other's well-being. But all that changed so fast. Fortune shone on us and we suddenly got rich. With that you began avoiding us. Now my husband seldom spends the nights at home. He is all day at his work and spends the nights at the Baba's ashram. This will be the forty-seventh continuous day that he will not have spent the night at home. I used to share these things with Shakeela, hoping she would tell you about them and I would get at least a few words of concern from you for support. But you have all the while preferred to look the other way."

"Shakeela kept me informed of whatever you were sharing with her and I felt sincerely concerned about your plight," I responded. "Only that I didn't want to appear a meddlesome neighbour by discussing them with you. It would also look very improper, especially when Murari is continuously absenting himself from home."

"It's especially because he is continuously absenting himself that I need your emotional support. He thinks that all his wife and children need is wealth. He doesn't have any time to spend with the children. His official duty and business interests take up the whole day and he spends the nights at Baba's ashram. He says his business invariably suffers on the day following every night that he spends away from the ashram. He plays a father to the children and a husband to me through the phone, that's all."

"Has his business really suffered when he spends the nights outside Baba's ashram?"

"He enumerates countless instances to me when I protest that it's all just a superstitious belief."

"I never guessed things had gone so far. It's a pathetic situation. Should I talk to Murari?"

"Your talking to him will not be of any help," she sighed. "He will not change his ways. He is that addicted to riches. I keep telling him we have plenty and enough is enough, but he says all that we have could vanish within days if he doesn't spend his nights at Baba's ashram."

"Money has this vicious grip on man," I said, shifting to the philosophic. "The more you get, the more you will want. Murari is a helpless victim. He, surely, won't be happy staying away from home. Why don't you ask him to build a spacious house near Baba's ashram so that you could move there? As it is, your small apartment doesn't suit you anymore."

"I have been making that suggestion to him whenever I get a chance to talk to him, but he is not willing to disobey *vaastu* pandits who have, without exception, told him that luck will desert us the moment we vacate our apartment."

"It's a very sad and ironic situation. Fortune is forcing you to live apart."

"This loneliness in killing me, Shreeman," she wailed.

"Only divine intervention can help. You must invoke Goddess Saraswati's help to save Murari from the grip of Mammon. The goddess is most powerful at her shrine in Chinchal. I suggest you and the children go on a pilgrimage there. I shall also pray for you."

"I have spent most of my nights in vigil praying to all the gods and goddesses. They have not bothered to help me. They must be ridiculing me for asking them to make my husband stop amassing riches when millions of wives are daily pestering them for just the opposite."

"You're right, gods and goddesses only give blessings, they don't take them away. Maybe, the only choice for you then is to approach a demon. But I don't think the crisis is so serious as to seek a demon's intervention."

"It is enough that you intervene," she said. Her hands stretched out and grasped mine. "Shreeman, riches have made me desolate. I need you."

Her brimming eyes elicited a rush of sympathy from mine. They too filled.

"What can I do to help you?" I asked, oozing genuine concern.

"Just now, I need you," she said, and the next moment her lips pressed against mine.

Until then, my life had been one of surprises all through, but this one beat all. We shifted to my bed and spent an hour together, I becoming Murari for her and she becoming Shakeela for me. At the end of the unfamiliar experience of sleeping with a neighbour's wife – or, rather, my bete noir's wife – my emotions were as varied as the colours of the rainbow, spinning at an incredible speed to form that colourless shade called white. Yes, I was dead pale when Mrs Murari got up and gave me a parting kiss. "The children have gone for a matinee show with the servants. They will return in a few minutes," she said, and walked away.

The phone rang just then. I picked it up casually. It was Shakeela calling.

"How are you?" she asked.

"I'm fine."

"Hope you aren't skipping your meals. I know you'll rather go hungry than prepare something yourself. Forget about entering the kitchen. Eat at a good restaurant. Don't pinch on food. I lose my appetite the moment I sit at the table thinking you might be going about on a hungry stomach."

She was right. I preferred going hungry to entering the kitchen. If Shakeela weren't at home, I would sustain myself on a single meal. As for eating at a restaurant, I considered it an unforgivable extravagance. In fact, I hadn't eaten lunch that day. It was another matter that Mrs Murari had made good by feeding me with manna-from-heaven.

"I'm looking after myself well. You needn't worry about that. Aren't you coming the day after tomorrow?"

"Dad's health is suddenly gone a little worse. He is insisting I stay on here for a few days more. I haven't agreed."

"Now that he is so old, it would be unfair to deny him his wish."

"Can I stay on then?" There was joyful surprise in her tone. I had been strict with her only about one thing, and that was about staying away from home for long. The maximum I would agree to was a two-day stay with her kin twice or thrice a year.

"You can if you wish," I answered.

"For how many days more?"

"As long as you wish. Only, you should be back before

the school reopens for the children."

"That's three weeks."

"Okay, this time around you can stay for three weeks."

"Promise me you will look after yourself."

"I give you my word on that."

"Won't you miss me and the children?"

"You know I will, but dad is so old that it could just be the last vacation you and the children spend with him. We should not have to bear the endless pain of having denied him his last wish."

"Oh darling, how concerned you are for dad. Thank you so much. How I wish you were at hand for me to unburden the immense love I feel for you now. I am going to find it really hard to wait for two more weeks to hold you again in my arms. But, as you said, I should. It could just be the last chance I get to vacation with dad... Dad's calling. Bye!"

"I love you, darling."

She disconnected before I could get any hint that she had heard me.

Shakeela's words, their innocence and ardour, struck me with guilt. But I warded it off. She was happy staying with her parents; the children were happy playing with their cousins; Murari was happy sleeping in Baba's ashram; his children and servants were happy going to the matinee show daily; and Mrs. Murari and I were happy spending the afternoons making love. There could not have been a better arrangement. One could not plan and get such ideal situations. They had to happen just like that. And when they happened, they were a shot of great luck. And I for one strongly believed that I owed them to my new pets. And again, what better way to trample on Murari than by sleeping with his wife? My day had come at last!

Those were not the only arguments my mind spun to justify my sleeping with a neighbour's wife. There were more imaginative ones. Mrs Murari and I were two desolate souls who were finding refuge and fulfilment in each other. Shakeela used her veil time and again to slight me. Her devotion to the veil had distanced me from her more than I was aware of – not until Mrs Murari's blind devotion came my way did I become conscious of it. And as for Mrs Murari, her husband went after riches and abandoned her to loneliness. His devotion to Satsang Baba made her desolate. And so here were two unfortunate souls holding to each other and trying to survive. Who could say they were wrong?

I kept my word with Shakeela. I looked after myself well, or, rather, Mrs Murari looked after me well. She made sure that I ate good food. In fact, she did more by way of looking after my material needs than just feeding me well. She felt great pity that I did not have a car and home appliances, which I deserved by the sheer power of my magnanimous personality.

"Why did you sell them away?" she asked.

"The car I bought was a stolen one. I did not know that the man who sold me the car was a vehicle lifter. The police traced the car and returned it to its original owner."

"And didn't the vehicle lifter return your money?"

'Thieves aren't that decent. The police were worse. I had to give all the money and jewellery I had to them just not to get implicated in a theft case. The vehicle lifter used the same blackmail and took away the TV, fridge, air conditioners and every other valuable he saw in this house."

"How sad! You should buy a new car and all that you lost soon."

"I'm spending quite a bit of my salary buying lottery tickets, hoping against hope that I'll win a bumper prize soon."

"You have already won it. Come with me, I'll show you how much it is."

She rose and led me into her apartment. I followed her, bewildered by what seemed to be a cranky revelation. She went into her bedroom. I followed her into it. She removed the bedcover. Below was just a quilt. She removed the quilt. Below were stacked bundles of thousand-rupee notes. The cot itself was a two feet deep six-feet-by-six-feet coffer. I gaped and stood dumb-stuck. I felt swimmy.

"I shall show you more," Mrs Murari said, and led me into the pooja room. She removed the large pictures of gods and goddesses that covered the room's walls and pulled out deep hidden drawers. They were all stacked with thousand-rupee notes. She took me to her kitchen and showed me the huge amount of cash that was hidden there. She led me back into her bedroom. She pulled the quilt back on to the rupee-note wads. We sat on a two feet thick bed of notes. "This house has many more hollows stacked with notes," she said. "I am sitting guard here over something around five billion rupees. When Murari comes next, he will bring at least twenty million more. There isn't much space left to stack them in. Take as much money as you want and buy the richest car and the best of luxuries. So much money is flowing into this house that your requirements are not going to deplete its coffers any considerable bit."

Was I dreaming? All that I saw and heard was so much like a mirage. How did Murari get so much money? Wasn't it a risk to stock so much money in his house? And why was Mrs Murari so foolishly open and generous with me just because I shared bed with her a few times? It was all too weird to be true.

"Fear not, darling," she said, holding me close. "Murari is not going to find out even if you take away a quarter of the money. He no more keeps an account of the money kept here. That work is left to me. The more he brings, the greater becomes my burden. The first hundred thousand he brought five years ago had me in ecstasy. I had not seen so much money before. When money began to come in an incessant flow and thousands became millions and millions become billions, it became for me a constant source of anxiety and an unbearable burden. Now it also causes me revulsion. May be I am feeling so because it has alienated me from the hard work, little hassles and pinches of life that I had got addicted to, or it could be because it took away the simple and happy existence I enjoyed together with my husband. Just as it began suffocating and driving me mad, you came into my life and rescued me. What a relief I feel after opening the coffers and laying bare their contents to you. I regained my lost life and am able to breathe easy again. You made it possible, dear. I love you." She kissed me.

"How did Murari make so much money so fast?"

"By the power of Satsang Baba. It was five years ago that he went to have his first *darshan* of the Baba. At the end of Baba's public *darshan*, he was chosen for the special night darshan of the Baba, which is given only to one devotee a day. That night *darshan* was the turning point. Baba gave him a bundle of ten thousand rupees at the end of the *darshan* and asked him to invest it in the shares of a particular company. The value of the shares doubled in two days. He went back to Baba. Baba gave him the special night *darshan* again and asked him to sell the shares and invest the money in the shares of another company. The value of those shares doubled the very next day. The bull was charging and jumping high walls then. He went daily to have Baba's *darshan* then on and he stayed in Baba's ashram till midnight. Money multiplied like splitting amoeba."

I was tempted to forego her kisses and rush to the Baba for a night *darshan*, but she was holding me so tight that I just couldn't bring myself to doing so. Instead, I asked, "And when the market crashed...?"

"Baba warned him a week earlier that the crash was coming. He sold off all the shares he had, after which Baba went on a European tour and Murari spent a few nights at home. The market bottomed out by the time Baba returned from his foreign tour and Murari went back to the ashram. The night *darshan*s were again reserved for him. Baba advised him at each *darshan* which shares to buy. The market shot up from 2600 points to 5900 points within two months, taking flight on the rumour that the Pokran nuclear blasts had frightened the gulf countries into selling oil to India at half the market prize. Baba then advised Murari to sell off all the shares. Ten billion came in just two weeks. The market crashed once again when it became clear that the gulf countries did nothing to give meat to the rumour that shot the market up and, instead, the rich and industrialised countries clamped crippling sanctions on India. The market continues to rise and fall like the waves in a storm, bringing in billions a year."

"Does the Baba give *darshans* in the evening?"

"Why? You want to have his *darshan*?"

"Yes. If possible, I want to have his *darshan* this evening itself."

"No, dear, you must not have his *darshan*. I do not want to risk losing you too. I'll give you all the money you need."

She stretched herself on the bed and pulled me down on to her. We made love lying on Murari's notes.

Truly, when God gives, he gives with abandon. I bought a better car than Murari's – with his money. I bought a better brand of all the luxury appliances he had at home – with his money. Murari slogged the whole day and spent lonely nights at Baba's ashram while I enjoyed his wife and his money. Was there any better way I could claim victory over him? There wasn't any I could think of. But there was no question of my ruling out the possibility of something more spectacular suddenly turning up as long as I took good care of my pets.

I bought the latest model BMW, a blue one, because Mrs Murari liked blue. I also bought the home appliances the same day, all blue. Although I talked long with Shakeela daily on the phone, I did not tell her about the car or the appliances for the simple reason that I wasn't sure she would take it well. Each day she sounded as eager as Mrs Murari to get into my arms. I just hoped that, by the time she returned home, her longing for me would grow strong enough to make her acquiesce in my purchases. If she were to ask me how I got the money, I had the answer ready. But something still kept nagging me. Was it the fear that, with Shakeela returning home, my trysts with Mrs Murari would come to an end? No, I didn't have to fear on that count: My new spacious car would be a convenient love-nest. I would pick Mrs Murari up from a predetermined place in the city and drive to a remote place and we would make love to the bucolic tunes of shepherds' flutes. What was it then that made me more and more apprehensive as the day of Shakeela's return neared? Yes, that was it. Shakeela's nose. Wouldn't she smell out my affair with Mrs Murari and all the hush-hush treachery that went with it? There was every chance she would. I had to take some precaution urgently.

The only way out for me was to scotch Shakeela's nose. I had to somehow destroy its power to smell out what goes on in other people's minds. I would have to take the help of a tantrist for that. I had not had any dealing with tantrists before and I dreaded approaching one now. Perhaps, Sampat Iyer could help. I went to him one evening.

"My wife has the extraordinary power to smell out whatever goes on in my mind," I explained. "It's creating untold problems between us. She questions me always about my thoughts and sentiments. Her meddlesome nose gets on my nerves all the time and I often get mad at her. There is never peace in the house."

"Your wife must have been born on a Total Solar Eclipse day, just at the moment when the spectacular phenomenon of the Diamond Ring occurs. People born at that rare moment have the rare power to smell out what works in other people's minds."

"Is there a way to snuff out the special power of her nose?"

"To be frank, there is little people like me can do about it. A Diamond Ring is such a rare phenomenon that its effects can be nullified only by tantrists who have acquired perfect control of the five elements. There are hardly a dozen tantrists who have reached that state. There is one Maharaj Trishankmurthy whom you could approach."

"Where does he stay?"

"Not very far from here. The problem with him is that he charges a hefty fee."

"Money won't be a problem provided he disciplines my wife's nose."

"Nasty noses are small fry for him. He'll do the job in minutes, but his minimum fee is fifty thousand."

Sampat Iyer expected he would give me a start by mentioning so big a sum. Little was he aware that I had any mount of Murari's money at my disposal. I agreed for the amount, despite my suspicion that he would appropriate half of it as his cut of the fee.

On the morrow, Maharaj Trishankmurthy trapped Shakeela's uncanny sense of smell in a snuff box and threw it into a pond. I had to pay twenty thousand extra for doing it in Shakeela's absence.

It was Shakeela who would ring me up every day. That evening, three days before she and the children were to return, I gave her a surprise and rang her up.

"How is dad?" I asked.

"He is in fine shape now. He says he feels a few years younger. I am so glad I could tend him back to good health."

"And God has immediately rewarded us for it. We have landed a windfall."

"A windfall? What's it?"

"Guess."

"You got a promotion?"

"No."

"Your father gave you another piece of cobra-infested land?"

"No, something much bigger than that."

"I can't guess. I give up."

I got the first clear indication that Maharaj Trishankmurthy had scotched her nose.

"I won a lottery."

"For how much?"

"Guess."

"A hundred thousand?"

"Your guess is too low."

"A million?"

"The ten-million Diwali Bumper."

There was no response.

"Shakeela, Shakeela," I called out.

There was no response again. The phone was not disconnected.

"Shakeela, Shakeela," I called out again.

There was still no response. There was something seriously amiss. I got panicky. I should not have conveyed so stunning a news over the phone. Had she swooned? No, that might not have been the case, because I had not heard any disturbance through the phone. I continued to call out to her. A minute passed and still there was no response. What was I to do now? Rush to her, what else? I was plucking the receiver off my ear when I heard her say, "God has been so kind to us, dear."

"What happened? Why did the phone go silent for so long?" I asked, still disturbed.

"I was saying a silent prayer thanking God."

"Couldn't you have prayed aloud?"

"I was so happy I could hardly open my mouth."

"So, it was almost as I guessed. Anyway, listen carefully to what I have to say. Don't share this news with anybody, not even with your parents."

"It's such a big piece of news, how can I keep it back

from them?"

"You'll have to, or we will get into great troubles. Just like you, your parents will find it hard to keep it back from your brothers and sisters. That way it will spread like wild fire and set the income tax authorities on our heals in no time. They will take away forty percent of the money."

"But isn't that inevitable?"

"There is a way out if we can keep it a secret. We can sell the ticket to Murari for one-and-a-half times its value. He will use it to change his black money into white."

"Does he have so much money?"

"It's a paltry amount for him. I came to know the other day that he has at least five billion in cash with him."

No response. A long pause. I had blundered again. I should not have mentioned so huge a sum to her. This time I had to wait for five minutes to hear her again.

"Thank God, dear," she said. "He has been so good to our neighbour."

"Did you have to take so long to thank God for giving Murari so much money?"

"I prayed for our intentions too. I was praying God to make us feel contented with the ten million he has given us and not to be in agony because it is nothing compared to the billions the Muraris have."

"I don't feel envy towards them anymore. I now take it as though what the Muraris have is also ours. Believe me, I have changed a lot while you were tending dad."

"May the good God be praised! The change that has come about in you is a greater fortune than the ten-million lottery."

Well, she was in fact confirming a third favour, a greater one than the other two – she could no more smell out what was going on in my mind. I imitated her and prayed silently for a few seconds and thanked God. When I restarted the conversation, I realised she had hung up. She might have thought her remark had offended me and I had disconnected. It, sure, would not have appeared to her that I had paused to thank God for a big favour.

In the end, I was happy that I had spun a credible story for the money Mrs. Murari had put at my disposal.

I went in my brand new car and brought Shakeela and the children home. To my great surprise, she took my pricey purchases well. She took them as God-given blessings. She had a greater surprise in store for me – she did not wear the veil when we stepped out of home after her return.

"Did you forget to wear the veil?" I asked.

"I have decided not to wear it anymore. It was to make you realise your mistakes that I wore the veil again. The fortune God has given us now is the proof that you have accepted your mistakes and wept over them. God is much pleased with you. Why should I then continue to wear the symbol of my protest?"

That was a shocking anticlimax. This time around, I wanted her to wear the veil. It was the sole excuse I had to practice treachery on her. Now that she has discarded the veil, I would not have the guts to sleep with Mrs Murari again.

"It's so heartening to hear that you believe I have become my old self again," I said. "In turn, let me confess that your veil does play an indispensable role in making me continue to be so. Your voluntary offer to discard the veil gives me immense joy. For this joy to remain with me, it is important that you should continue to wear the veil. It will hold me from slipping back into my mistakes." I led her back into the house.

I took out the veil from the wardrobe and put it on her. I bought two more veils for her to impress on her that I meant what I said.

Chapter - 5

Satsang Baba

I am not one to leave things halfway. I was riding piggyback on Murari, like the bird that perches proudly on a buffalo's back. But, in comparison, I was so small. I wouldn't rest till I became something bigger than Murari, say an elephant compared to Murari the buffalo. Only Satsang Baba could make me so big. But my mind recoiled at the thought of approaching Baba. I still entertained a grudge against him for having turned the tables on me at Murari's wedding anniversary. But I had to forgive and forget if I must achieve my ultimate goal of becoming richer and bigger than Murari.

I planned a secret trip to Baba's ashram, situated about a hundred kilometres away. I told Shakeela and Mrs Murari that I was going on an official tour for a few days and timed the tour to coincide with Murari's hospitalisation with a serious attack of hepatitis.

I travelled by bus to Baba's town. The bus took three hours to cover the distance. I knew very little about Baba's life and miracles. I was definitely aware that he had a vast following. He had devotees from every stratum of society and every nation. He was the favourite godman of rich businessmen and powerful politicians. The poignant facts about him that I knew were gathered from his appearance at Murari's party and those that Murari had told me about. I thought it was only right and fair that I studied more about him before I met him. So I carried a biography of his and read it on the bus. A British disciple of his had written it.

I read it at a stretch till the bus' tires plunged into a pothole, throwing me up to the roof of the bus for the first time. By then I had learned that Baba had an extraordinary birth. His mother brought him forth at midday sharp. The sun turned crimson, cattle flocked to the compound of the house of his birth and birds congregated on the roof above. He came out in a squatting posture, and when the nurse held him and hit him on his buttocks, he laughed instead of crying. Koyals joined in and sang their hearts out as peacocks performed a Kathakali number to their tune. And when he cried at last for milk, a cow rushed in, lifted its hind leg and squirted milk from its udder directly into his mouth. The sun did not set for three days, until he commanded it to set with a wave of his tiny hand.

Baba's childhood also was extraordinary. At three months, he recited the Vedas by heart, and at six months he started giving discourses to his mother. The first discourse he gave was about family planning, quoting revelations profusely from the holy books of different religions on the subject. He also recited many enigmatic *slokas* which contained prophecies about important events. One of the first prophetic *slokas* he uttered was this: 'The Great Serpent shall smoulder and *Saki* shall burn alive.' The Sanskrit word for serpent is *naga*. Baba's disciples who were delving into his obscure prophecies (Baba's divinity restrained him from himself explaining them) joined *naga* to *Saki* and the missed prophesy got revealed forty years after Naga*saki* was burned alive by a nuclear bomb.

Baba started walking very late. He was six when he took his first step.

I was taking a break to meditate over these facts when the bus plunged into the next pothole and threw me up, this time strongly enough to make my head bulge. I massaged the bulge and read on. The chapter on Baba's boyhood was short. He fled to the nearby forest and took refuge in a cave at the age of ten. There he sat squatting for six years, not shifting once. He only had to open his mouth when he felt hungry. Cows took turns to squirt milk into his mouth and birds took turns to drop fruits in and bees took turns to inject honey. Peacocks spread out their tails and fanned him when it got warm and bears hugged him when it became cold. Elephants brought water in their trunks and bathed him, and monkeys preened his copious hair.

The bus did not plunge into potholes anymore, because the road became wide and smooth halfway to Baba's ashram. The smooth ride lilted me into a doze and I closed the book. But the man next to me had overtaken me and was plunging about in deep sleep. He kept on hitting my shoulder with his head. When his head hit my head, I thought I had rather sit awake and read Baba's biography than get hit again. I skipped a few chapters and read the fascinating one on Baba's miracles. It was a long chapter. I will just mention here a few sample miracles.

Baba worked his first public miracle on the day he came out of the forest and walked into his village at the age of eighteen. A severe drought was on then. Crops were withering and the people were weeping. Baba sat in the middle of the vast expanse of dying crops and played the flute, which Krishṇa had one night appeared and presented to him. All the animals from miles around flocked to the fields – there were thousands of them – and urinated time and again till the fields were slightly soaked. Some life returned to the crops. Baba continued to play the flute. Towards nightfall, the sky became overcast and, within minutes, it rained cats and dogs. The animals dispersed; not a bite did they take of the crops.

Here is another astounding miracle Baba performed later in life, when he had ascended from the *sanyasa* state of the cave to the nirvana state of the air-conditioned luxury car. He was on a visit to Madras. The Chief Minister's motorcade had caused a three-kilometre long traffic jam. Baba got stranded at the tail end. He waived his right hand, and lo, all the vehicles there, including the Chief Minister's car, rose to the air and stood suspended above. Baba swished past in his car on a free road, hurling blessings on the devotees who worshiped him from above. The next day, the peeved Chief Minister presented a helicopter to Baba, which he has been using ever since for his inland travels.

Another miracle, which I must not fail to mention, because it was of great national importance, took place during the Indo-Pak war of 1971. In fact, the miracle gave victory to India and concluded the war. Nixon sided with Pakistan and sent the Seventh Fleet into the Bay of Bengal to threaten India. Rattled, Indira Gandhi rushed to Baba. He smiled and told her to take it cool. He told the Prime Minister to fight the war to the finish and assured her that he would take care of Nixon and his Seventh Fleet. Baba sat in *Yuddhasana* and prayed. Within minutes, the propellers of all the ships of the Seventh Fleet went dead. The fleet stood still. Nixon got exasperated and ordered the fleet to shower missiles on India. Not one missile fired. Nixon ordered a tactical retreat and sent other ships to tow the Seventh Fleet back to the Pacific Ocean. India won the war. The author of the biography went on to lament that an ungrateful nation did not include this great feat of the Baba, which gave it its first military victory in many centuries, in the time capsule that Indira Gandhi sent down into the womb of the earth.

Perhaps Baba worked his most fascinating miracle high above in the sky. It happened when the Defence Minister was taking him along the Indo-Pak border in an Air-Force fighter plane. Despite the ingratitude his country had shown after his miraculous intervention during the 1971 war, Baba volunteered to deaden the surface-to-air missiles Pakistan had deployed along the border. He was doing exactly that, sitting in *Yuddhasana* in the Air-Force plane, when a Pak fighter plane approached and fired a missile at it. Baba stretched his hand out of the plane and snatched the missile before it hit its target. He then hurled it at the Pak plane in which Zia-ul-Haq was simultaneously flying. That was the end of Zia-ul-Haq. The Pakistanis were still pretending to be clueless about the accident that killed their president, because they were unwilling to publicly acknowledge Baba's supernatural powers.

The simplest miracle Baba worked was this: He placed his hand on the tummy of a childless woman who was past menopause and made her pregnant. He worked the miracle during the special night *darshan* he gave her. The child the woman gave birth to was now a disciple of Baba.

The bus stopped near the gate of Baba's ashram for the devotees to disembark. I was awestruck by the grandiosity of the ashram. It was a huge marble-wrapped building of palatial grandeur. I felt swimmy, just like when Mrs Murari had laid bare her husband's hidden treasure to me. The devotee had to become insignificant if he was to get filled with Baba's divinity and grow big. As I stood facing the magnificent structure, I became as insignificant as a speck of dust. There was so much money and opulence in divinity!

Construction of the grandiose ashram had thrown the only two challenges Baba had faced to his divinity yet. The first one came from the contractor who built the ashram. The man had inherited the notion from our forefathers that it was unprofessional to complete and handover a building within the agreed time. Baba, who had imbibed bits of alien managerial culture and ethics from his foreign followers, was enraged at seeing just the skeleton of the ashram completed a week before the day he was to move into it.

"You must complete the building in three days or quit!" Baba decreed.

The contractor replied with a wry smile which said, "Godmen by definition are cranky, but you are a lunatic."

Baba thundered, "I'll come after three days. The building should be ready for occupation or you should have vacated this place by then. I hope I have made myself clear!"

The contractor retorted, "Why wait for three days when

it is in your power to complete the building in a second by simply wishing it? Perform the miracle and I shall return all the money I have taken from you."

"You shall not tempt the Lord your God," Baba quoted Jesus, and wriggled out.

The contractor was given six more months to complete the building.

The ashram building occasioned the second major challenge to Baba's divinity during its inaugural ceremony. Baba produced a gold chain out of thin air and presented it to the architect who had designed the ultramodern ashram. One of Door*darshan*'s cameras covering the programme caught a disciple red-handed in the act of offering the chain clandestinely to Baba on a platter. As luck would have it, the Information and Broadcasting Minister, under whose charge Door*darshan* came, was a protégé of Baba. The minister confiscated and destroyed the tape before it fell into the hands of Baba's baiters.

The divinity Baba exhibited in warding off the challenges attracted thousands more to him.

I entered the huge archway that welcomed thousands of devotees every day. Inside the ashram premises, everything was spick-and-span, smart and solemn, orderly and quiet, as in a military camp. I flowed with the current into the *darshan* hall. It was a spacious hall with a very high roof. There were no impeding columns. The hall was nearly filled with devotees, squatting in rows and waiting for Baba to appear. There were people of every continent and race among them. It was a heavenly gathering. The devotees faced a golden throne placed on a rostrum. The throne was crafted in the model of the legendary Peacock Throne. There was half-an-hour more for the *darshan*, but everyone sat in perfect silence, eagerly waiting for Baba to appear.

I squatted and daydreamed about the favours I could obtain from Baba. The first important thing was that I should ingratiate myself with him and secure a special night *darshan*. And for that, I sat in the front row with folded arms and supplicant eyes. I would not return home till Baba granted me the exclusive night *darshan*, during which I would be alone with him and I could make my requests. What specific requests should I make and how was I to put it to him? My purpose was to multiply money and get richer than Murari, at the wink of an eye if possible. I had a major advantage over Murari: He had come to Baba empty-handed while I had lots of his money at my disposal. I did not have to start with a paltry ten thousand rupees. I could start with a billion, thanks to Mrs Murari.

But was it prudent to tell Baba that I had so much money to start the multiplication game? It would be absurd to do so. How was I then to make the request? I just could not think of a winnable strategy. A sense of despondency began to neigh me down. I came to the conclusion that I had made a hopeless trip and thought of getting out. Then, suddenly, I got a brainwave. After all, I wouldn't have to make a request. Baba could read everything that went on in a devotee's mind. I smiled. But soon I realised that I had come against a bigger predicament. Would not Baba find out that it was a sinful desire to overtake Murari that had brought me to him? Murari was his favourite devotee. Would he condone the envy I entertained towards someone who was so dear to him? Wouldn't the all-knowing Baba find out that I had appropriated Murari's wife and money? Wouldn't he know that I was entertaining a grudge against him for what he had done to me at Murari's wedding anniversary party and was longing to pay him back? Wouldn't he react by punishing me with a curse? I was ruined! What a catastrophe I was inviting by seeking Baba's special *darshan*! I better abandon my mission and get away before Baba makes his appearance.

As I was rising to get away, I heard a roar. "Om Baba, Satsang Baba; Om Baba, Satsang Baba; Om Baba, Satsang Baba," the devotees chanted in unison till Baba, who appeared and seated himself on the golden throne, motioned with his hand to the hysteric crowd to fall silent. I slumped back to the floor, crawled a few feet back and made a strenuous effort, shifting this way and that, to hide myself from Baba's eyes behind those who sat in front. Luckily,

Baba seldom looked in my direction.

A devotee stood on the rostrum and sang a *bhajan*:

'I come to you, sage, a humble seeker,
You have all the answers, godly seer,
Stranded I stand in the middle of life,
Troubling questions hold my soul in deep strife,
In a desert lost, I look back and forth,'
'For the start 'n the finish; where is the north?

'You count dust to know the vastness of land,
You'll not reach the rainbow band with your hand.
You count drops to know the stretch of oceans,
You've small vision; only can see portions.
You dismember each man to find his soul,
You discard the seen for the unseen goal.

'You ask: whence do I come? Where do I go?
From a womb you came with little to show,
Into six foot womb you'll go in the end.
Neither you began nor ever will end.
To your mother by birth, you were her heart,
In death, mother earth will make you her part.

'You see parrots fly above the high pine,
And ask: In what colour does the Lord shine?

Orange, violet, red, blue, yellow or green?
Close your eyes, look within and see the sheen
Of things small 'n big, ugly 'n pretty, low 'n high.
When you nameless brilliance see, it is I.'

A disciple of Baba then appeared and made an announcement. "Baba will answer your doubts," he said. "You may ask any question you may have on spiritual matters. Don't make any request for favours. Baba knows you have come to seek some and His Holiness also knows the favours each one is seeking without your telling him. You will have received the favours by the time you reach back home if Baba feels that you deserve them and they will do you good. Now is the occasion for you to receive enlightenment from His Holiness on the only thing that really matters, the well-being of your soul."

The disciple disappeared through a side door. There was a long pause during which Baba searched in vain for someone who would raise his or her hand. Then a lady with Mongolian features raised her hand. Baba signalled to her with his hand to go ahead and ask her question. She stood up and asked, "What shall I do, Baba, to enjoy uninterrupted happiness?"

"There is only one way you can enjoy uninterrupted and pure happiness," Baba said, "it is to divest yourselves of all desires. If you have no desires, you will have no disappointments. Happiness is the state of mind one enjoys when one has no disappointments."

"Won't I cease to be human if I have no desires?" the woman asked.

"You cannot be fully human and happy at the same time."

The woman sat down not-so-humanly satisfied.

"An African and an Indian raised their hands. Baba motioned to the African to speak. He asked, "Baba, I would like to have a clarification on what you said. Happiness is a positive experience that comes from a feeling of fulfilment. How can it be achieved by the negation of something?"

"I am happy you asked the question," Baba replied. "It shows you are on the path to true knowledge and have reached a stage where it is possible for you to put poignant questions. For the achievement of happiness, which means becoming one with the ultimate divine reality, shedding your desires alone will not suffice. You will also have to seek the fulfilment of heavenly aspirations."

The African did not exactly catch the point. He sat down, preferring to be positively unhappy than negatively happy.

It was now the turn of the Indian, someone from the north of the Vindhyas, to make a query. "Is there a life after death?" he asked.

"There is and there is not," Baba promptly answered.

"For those who die to their self, there is a life after death. Their souls escape from their mortal bodies even while they live. So their souls do not die when their mortal bodies perish. Those others whose souls remain trapped in their bodies while they live will not have life after death, because their souls will perish with their bodies."

The wheat coloured Indian took his seat, apparently happy with the answer he got. I was happy with him. I felt reassured that my soul would not outlive my body and be cast into hell for the envy I was having for Murari and for the sins I was committing with his wife.

There was a rush to ask questions, but Baba signalled an end to the session after he answered six more questions.

Baba stood up. The congregation stood up.

"Sing with me by repeating after me each line of the *bhajan* I'll sing," Baba said.

Baba sang a Mira *Bhajan* and the congregation sang along. Baba swayed his head; the devotees swayed their heads. Baba raised his hands; the devotees raised their hands. Baba raised his eyes towards heaven; the devotees raised their eyes towards heaven. Baba swayed his body; the devotees swayed their bodies. Baba went into a trance; the devotees went into a trance. Baba pranced; the devotees pranced. The roar of the *bhajan* hit the roof and pierced it through, letting heaven in. Baba's face shone like the sun; the devotees saw a heavenly vision. Baba's soul left his body for a moment and flew up, throwing him prone on the ground; the souls of the devotees left their bodies and lay prone on the ground. Baba's soul returned to his body and he rose; the souls of the devotees returned to their bodies and they rose. Baba sat on the throne; the devotees squatted on the floor.

There appeared a bright new halo around Baba's head. Devotees went to Baba one by one and lay prone in front of him. Baba placed his right foot on each devotee's head and, at that moment, a bright new halo appeared around the head of the devotees. It was a heavenly experience for the devotees, but it was the contrary for me. It unmistakably brought home to me the supernatural powers of Baba and frightened the life out of me. He would read my treacheries and punish me! I wanted to rush out and catch the first bus home, but the door was closed and would not open until Baba signalled the end of the *darshan*. After the last devotee was thus invested with the halo, Baba waded through the congregation to select the lucky one who would get his special *darshan* that night. I looked down to avoid giving him my face. I dreaded getting exposed by him. I had only one thing in mind – to rush out. I would remain satisfied with siphoning off the money Murari amassed. After all, Murari's wife slept with me more often than with him, and that was no mean victory I could claim over him, though it was purely a private satisfaction that could not be flaunted in public.

Baba came and stood near me for a while. My soul fluttered, fearing it was going to fly off from my mortal body forever. I shivered violently as I made a herculean effort to hold it back. Baba moved away. My soul quietened and my body became still. Baba did not select anyone for the night *darshan*. Perhaps he would give it to the same devotee who had got it the previous night but was not present at the public *darshan*. That might have been how Murari got it so often. I breathed easy as Baba walked back to the rostrum. Baba sat on his throne and motioned to the devotees with both his hands to rise and disperse. I made it to the door first. As the door was opening, Baba's voice came through the public address system, "The devotee who reached the door first will have my special *darshan* tonight." Life went out of me for a few seconds. When I got it back by the grace of Baba, three saffron-clad disciples of Baba had surrounded me. They led me away to Baba's private quarters.

I was accommodated in a well-furnished room that had all the modern comforts. I was attended to like a prince. The special attention I got did little to lessen my apprehension that Baba had picked me up for the night *darshan* to confront me with the grudge I bore him and the treachery I was committing on Murari, his favourite devotee. My envy for Murari had made him my life's obsession, bringing me fortunes and misfortunes, favours and fears, through unpredictable quirks of fate. Into what frightening misery was it going to drive me next? Oh no, I wouldn't need to have such fears as long as no harm came to my new pets. They would keep my life on a fortunate course. But would the stars of the pets have the power to control Baba, whose divinity was beyond the control of astrology or any such thing? No! I was doomed! I had lost count of the number of times I had slept with Mrs Murari; But the all-knowing Baba would know even that detail. He would even know how many times I had committed adultery with her on my bed, how many times on Murari's bed, and how many times in the car I had bought with Murari's money. And if Baba asked me how much of Murari's money I had taken in return for substituting him as his wife's bedfellow, I wouldn't exactly know, But Baba would know the amount to the smallest change. What would come of me if Baba pronounced a curse for each occasion I slept with Mrs. Murari? I could turn to a miserable worm. And what if he pronounced one big curse for the money I took? It could squash half of me and only one half of me would be allowed to wriggle out! Night was approaching. I closed my eyes and wished to seek refuge in Shakeela's veil, imagining that I was hiding myself in it.

I opened my eyes only when I heard a loud knock at the door. It was ten in the night. It was a call for the exclusive *darshan*. I was led into the luxuriously furnished bedroom of Baba and was left alone with him. Baba welcomed me with a beaming smile. He put his arm around me and led me to a chair by the side of his bed. He sat on the bed. He looked into my eyes, still smiling. I shivered and looked away.

"Fear not, child!" he whispered, "Quieten your soul and look into my eyes."

I forced my eyes up. Baba's eyes beamed so friendly a gleam that mine remained glued to them.

"What's your name?"

"Shreeman."

"What favour do you want?"

The encounter was turning out to be so different from what I had feared it would be. Here was a golden opportunity to make the request for which I had set out to meet him. But was Baba laying a trap for me by asking the exact question I had wished he would ask? I dared not ask anything that Baba could contort to ask me questions about Murari. I sought an escape and swerved to the spiritual. I recited the only spiritual line I knew: "Lead me from ignorance to truth, from darkness to light, and from death to immortality."

"Blessed are you, for you asked what really matters. You are the first one to approach me with the all-inclusive quest and the right disposition. You will get what you asked, in full measure. I shall lead you from ignorance to truth, from darkness to light, and from death to immortality. You are asking the bliss of enlightenment, which is liberation, which is Brahman, which is *moksha*, which even the rishis achieved only after years of intense *tapasya*. Surrender yourself to me, for I am the Enlightened One, Parabrahman, the Supreme Godhead, and I shall deliver you straight away from the ocean of death-bound existence."

I had landed in something new and absorbing. I hadn't thought that the supernatural could be so exciting. I wanted to be led on.

"How should I surrender myself to you, oh Parabrahman?"

"You must shed your self, the 'I' in you, and come out of the bondage of Maya. It is the attachment to the self that makes you think that you are different from others, that man is different from God, that man is different from the world, that a man is different from a woman, that pleasure is different from bliss, that mind is different from the body. Attachment to the self is the fountainhead of Maya. It is Maya that differentiates between sin and virtue and causes guilt; Maya differentiates the ugly from the beautiful and makes you feel the shame; Maya differentiates pain from pleasure and makes you cry; Maya differentiates you from me and makes us sit apart."

I was full of shame, pain and guilt. I wanted to get rid of them all. Baba could do it if I drew close to him. He was Parabrahman, the Enlightened One, in whose proximity all my guilt, pain and shame would vaporise and disappear.

"What should I do to discard the self and escape from the bondage of Maya?"

"Come closer and erase the distance between you and me."

I drew near to him. He stood up and held me close.

"I am Parabrahman," Baba said, pressing me tight. "Allow me to posses you and your false self will evaporate. Remove all illusions of Maya and open up your *Atman* that I may enter therein. Shed the illusion of the artificial light and let darkness reign so that the divine light may enter." Baba switched off the lights.

"Undress and shed your shyness so that naked joy may seep into you." Baba undressed and undressed me. "Hold me tighter and shed your guilt so that you may enjoy unadulterated bliss." He pressed me tight and bliss made its entry between my thighs.

"Shed all preconceptions that differentiate man from God, man from woman and right from wrong." It was man and man, man with man, man on man, man into man, man into man, man into man, man into man, man into man..., man, man, man, man... till I felt the wetness of bliss.

Bliss depleted, Parabrahman lay exhausted. I lay by his side disgusted and humiliated. How despicable a situation envy had led me into! I ended up becoming the plaything of a cunning sex-maniac. What worse retribution for sexploiting my neighbour's wife? Would it all end there, or was something worse still coming? I was so dejected that I wanted to cry aloud for relief, but I couldn't. I lay blinking into the darkness.

After a while light came on and Baba spoke.

"You are very receptive to enlightenment, son. It will take many more special *darshans* for you to completely shed the self and all its bondages and inhibitions. Visit me as often as you can. The more often you come the sooner you will achieve liberation and the ultimate goal of endless bliss. Day by day you will get detached from possessions. When you will have reached the stage of complete detachment and perfect fulfilment in the divine, I shall give you riches in abundance and make you the richest among the rich. I shall make you so powerful that no one will ever dare challenge you. You may now dress up and go back to your room."

Back in my room, I considered the promises Baba had made. A lot of things suddenly fell into place and became clear to me. I understood how Murari had become Baba's favourite. Baba had just promised me that he would favour me as he did Murari and make me rich and powerful. Baba had used me. The only way to pay him back was to use him in turn, even if it meant I had to continue to be his plaything. He had in the first session itself taught me to consider my body a slough I should discard. Why was I to bother if he would use the slough as his plaything? And until I succeeded in sloughing off my body and self, I would mentally put on a veil while he used me. The veil joined hands with Advaita to deliver me out of the slough of despondence I was in. I would surrender myself to Baba and become richer and greater than Murari.

I was ebullient once again.

ജ്ഞജ്ഞ

I made steady progress in the path of enlightenment and supreme bliss. And as each special darshan of Baba honed my power of perception, I began to recognise the sounds of darkness. Soon, the duality of light and darkness got blurred and I saw the dubious activities of nocturnal cheats that the world around me bustled with. Baba lead me through the alleys of the mercenary world that thrived under the façade of his spiritual haven – an amazing web encompassing the whole world – and acquainted me with its language and culture.

It was a strange world where people gave away huge sums to others for insignificant favours. A Russian once gave a billion rupees to the Defence Minister just for flying in from Delhi to have tea with him at the ashram. On another occasion, a leading stockbroker gave fifty million to the chairman of Unit Trust of India just for spending an hour with him in prayer in a special room reserved for such VIPs. The Leader of the Opposition came one day and distributed twenty million each to eleven MPs who came to attend a prayer meeting that Baba himself conducted for invoking God's help to make him the Prime Minister. A Major General pecked an American lady's cheek while handing over a file and got ten million in return for the romantic gesture. The most unbelievable generosity was by an industrialist who gave the Minister for Heavy Industries fifty million for spending a night in the ashram with a call girl he arranged for the minister.

Baba got twenty-five percent of the money that changed hands thus, as rental for using the ashram's premises for performing the acts of generosity.

The stars of my pets had led me to the land of opportunities. I was confident I could flourish there and overtake Murari sooner than I had dreamt I would.

The farther I progressed, the more enriching and enchanting became my journey to enlightenment. I got hooked to Baba like an addict to cocaine. Baba gave me the high and I obeyed his commands.

I rang up Shakeela one fine morning.

"I'm afraid my work will hold me up here much longer than I expected," I told her, after exhausting husbandly pleasantries and enquiring after the children.

"Will you be held up for more than a week?" she asked, concerned.

"Can't really say. I'm working overtime to finish the work as fast as possible. It could still take a few weeks more."

"A few weeks more? You'll ruin your health if you eat at restaurants that long. Come home on weekends."

"I can do double the work on weekends. I'll finish the work and come. Don't worry; I'll take good care of myself."

"Sunil doesn't study a word. He sits glued to the TV watching cricket. He doesn't listen to me at all. The annual exams start next week. You will have to come if you want him to pass."

I could hear my son shout at his mother. I wanted to plead with him to take his studies seriously and promise him that I would take him to an international cricket match as a reward. Before I could ask Shakeela to give him the phone, he snatched the phone from her and came through.

"I have some great news for you, papa," he said, "Ravan has agreed to Pakistan and India playing a friendly test match here. The tickets we bought for the cancelled match will be valid for this match. You must come and take me to the match."

"When will the match be played?"

"It starts on the day after my exams get over."

"I'll take you to the test match on one condition; You must listen to mummy when she calls you to study."

"Agreed."

"Give mummy the phone."

Shakeela came on the line.

"Sunil has promised to listen to you."

"I doubt he will keep his word. He'll break any promise for the sake of cricket."

"He'll also keep any promise for the sake of cricket. I have promised to take him to the India-Pakistan friendly test if he keeps his word."

"It might work."

"It will."

"Ring up daily. Give me the number on which I can contact you in case of an emergency."

"I am touring around and so there isn't really a contact number I can give you. I shall ring you up as often as possible. How are the pets?"

"They're missing you. They've eaten very little after you left."

"Look after them well. I'll not delay a day longer than needed. Bye!"

I hung up.

That Ravan had changed his mind and come to my rescue was proof enough for me to believe that Baba had already started working wonders in my life. It was many days later that I came to know that the credit for the miracle should have gone to the Prime Minister who, in the national interest, gave one more berth to Ravan's party in the cabinet in return for the permission to conduct the match in our city. The Prime Minister was himself amply rewarded for the bold step he took. His popularity, which had sunk so low as to make his coalition partners think loudly of parting ways with him, shot up overnight and made his partners cling to him as fast as Baba had clung to me the previous few nights.

ജ്ഞ്ഞ

I rang up Mrs Murari six days later. Someone else took the phone and said 'hello'. I disconnected. I got her in person on the seventh attempt that evening, two hours before I was to get my special darshan of Baba.

"How are you, dear?" she asked, her voice betraying the immense pleasure my voice brought her.

"Fine. How are you?"

"Not as fine as when I had you with me."

"How is Murari?"

"His illness has developed serious complications. He has developed liver cirrhosis."

"That's a very serious condition. Didn't he ask you to take him to Baba? Baba could cure him with a mere touch of his hand."

"He hasn't made any such request yet. Maybe, he believes Baba knows everything and will intervene on his own if the doctors fail."

I had been on tenterhooks fearing that Murari would turn up at the ashram any time to meet Baba and find me there. The bugbear disappeared and I felt relaxed.

"What do the doctors say?"

"They are confident they can tackle his illness. They only caution that it could take some time."

"Ayurvedic medicines are very effective for treating such cases. Why don't you consult a *Vaidya*?"

"You stand hundreds of kilometres away and give me suggestions. Why don't you understand, I need you at my side for help? Please come back immediately."

I was so moved by her entreaty that I almost hung up to rush to her on the instant, but I controlled my emotions and held on to the phone.

"My work is now at a critical stage," I told her. "I shall complete it as fast as I can and rush to you."

"You can't imagine how lonely I feel, darling. Come to me this very moment if you can," she sobbed, and disconnected.

She was cut up, and I felt sad I had to disappoint her.

I had experienced a flush of elation when she told me that Murari's illness had got dangerously worse. I knew that there was a greater chance for him to succumb to the complication than survive it. It was plain envy that made my spirit bubble elation at the possibility of Murari's death.

On second thought, my envy became more ruthless and I wanted him to be alive while I became bigger than him. I prayed fervently for Murari's cure during Baba's public darshan.

The doctors fought Murari's illness successfully and he

got well in a month. The all-knowing Baba pretended he knew nothing about Murari's illness, perhaps because he was much engrossed in me.

I rang up Mrs Murari after a week. She transformed into a yearning gust over the phone and heaved me out of the ashram. We planned to meet at a hotel on the outskirts of the city. I hired a taxi and started immediately for the hotel. The car was a vintage model. I later learnt that the taximan had got it as dowry some thirty years ago. Half way through, it vomited, giving him the premonition that his wife had become pregnant for the sixteenth time. It laboured on for a couple of kilometres more till it had vomited out all its fuel.

I got pitiably stranded.

Vehicles sped by at long intervals, not paying any attention to my request for a lift. I would have had to wait for hours on end before I got a lift in some truck. The chance of my getting to Mrs. Murari before she lost her patience and went back home seemed too remote. I shouldn't have diluted my attachment to Baba by paying heed to Mrs. Murari's desire for me. I was going to pay the price for it by losing her forever. She wouldn't easily swallow my explanation that a breakdown of the taxi had prevented me from getting to her. No eager woman would ever accept such explanations. Despondent, I sat crouched on a small boulder, invoking the stars of my pets to come to my help, as the taximan waved at every passing vehicle for my sake.

Half-an-hour later, a truck carrying sand from a nearby river to the city responded to the taximan's waving and halted.

"Where to?" the driver asked.

"The city," I replied.

"Forty rupees," the driver said, quoting four times the fare one would usually have to pay.

"Okay," I said, allowing him to take advantage of my plight.

There was no space in the driver's cabin. I sat on the sand load.

I reached in time to take an exasperated Mrs Murari into my arms.

I had two more such rendezvous with Mrs Murari that week. She thanked me each time for the strength they gave her to face her husband's illness.

Chapter - 6

Border Dispute

The evening news-slot giving details about missing children, exhibiting their photos, brought me the news that my son had gone missing since four days. I rang up Shakeela to know the details, but no one was available at home. I ran to Baba and entreated his help. Baba assured me that my son was in no danger. He told me I had reached a stage of enlightenment where I was not to be told about the whereabouts of missing people. He directed me to go home and return as soon as I got my son back. Baba's tone gave me the impression that my son would have been traced by the time I reached home. Didn't Baba want me back the very next night?

When I reached home, my house had become an ocean

of tears. I tossed in it as Shakeela blurted out the story of our son's disappearance. I was so deeply engrossed in my journey to nirvana that I had forgotten about the promise I had made to my son about the friendly cricket test match between India and Pakistan. Early in the morning of the first day of the match, he ran down the stairs and shouted to his mother from below, flourishing the tickets I had bought for the abandoned test match, "I am going to the test match, mummy," and shot off to the road. Shakeela rushed down, but, by the time she reached the road, he had boarded a bus.

Shakeela had no way of contacting me (as days went by, my calls had become infrequent, because Baba was guiding me away from the world of wholesome attachments). Our neighbours formed squads and scoured the city and the cricket stadium for the boy. Murari used the substantial influence he wielded with the police and made maximum use of their network to search out my son. But all that did not help.

People whispered blood-chilling possibilities. The Chief Minister had laid the foundation for a new flyover in the city a day before the boy disappeared. I came to know it was a normal thing for contractors to sacrifice children to Goddess Kali before commencing such risk ridden projects. When a friend came to know that the rumour had reached my ears, he comforted me saying that only children below twelve were used for such human sacrifices. I wasn't really comforted, because my son had just crossed twelve. And very much unlike other children, he took pride in claiming to be younger than he was. If anyone asked his age, he would reply he was eleven. Another frightening rumour I heard was that a few gangs that kidnapped boys in their early teens were sneaking around the city. It was suspected that they were smuggling children across the border to Pakistan to sell them to the Taliban at an exorbitant price. I heard many more such weird rumours within hours of my reaching home. Each one hung like a millstone around my neck and added to my guilt. I would have to hold myself responsible for any tragedy that might befall my child. My selfish pursuits had forced me to neglect Shakeela and the children… No! There wasn't the need of my taking responsibility for my son's disappearance. Murari was finally to be blamed, not I. He had killed my pets and got rich, setting me on a path of unquenchable envy that landed me in so many tragic situations. Besides, my new pets and Baba would save the situation for me.

I went to my parrot with hands full of grains. It picked grains from my palms. I fed my cat with milk cupped in my hands. Reassured, I went out with Shakeela in search of our son.

We headed straight for the cricket stadium. We were sure that, if our son had belied the gruesome fears, he would come to the stadium. It was the final day of the test match and the tickets had been sold out. In fact, the stadium authorities had made a concession to the public mood and sold a hundred thousand tickets for a seventy thousand capacity stadium. The city was on fire with cricket craze and the tickets were consumed in minutes, mostly by flames that entered through the backdoor. Victory was in India's lap. India had a 187 lead and Pakistan had just one wicket in hand. Both the overnight batsmen were tail-enders. The game would most probably end with the first over of the day. Spectators knew as much. But they had come in full number to enjoy the thrill of the moment India would make Pakistan bite the dust. As for us, not getting entry into the stadium made no difference, because there was no meaning searching for our son in the huge overcrowded stadium within the little time Indian bowlers would need to make mincemeat of the Pakistanis.

We took our position on either side of a road through which pedestrians would have to pass after exiting the stadium. We waited anxiously for the deafening roar of victory and the bursting of crackers that would announce the end of the game. We did not hear them for a long time. Instead, there was the ominous silence of limbo, disturbed only by deep sighs of disappointment. The Indian bowlers were missing the wickets by hairline margins, I guessed. The sigh soon sounded alarming, giving me the firm indication that the game had taken a calamitous turn. I enquired of a traffic policeman, who was listening to the running commentary through the pocket radio he held close to his ear, about the progress of the game.

"The tail-enders are battering the Indian attack for sixes and fours," he moaned.

"How can that be?"

"Even tails can wag at loose balls and send them for sixes and fours."

"But aren't our ace bowlers bowling?"

"The Pakistanis must have performed black magic and crippled our bowlers."

"That's unfair."

"The Pakistanis will do anything to defeat India."

Only a few minutes were left for lunch break and the game was still on. The Pakistanis added a hundred and two runs more in the morning session. India experimented with all her bowlers in vain. Shakeela and I continued standing under the scorching sun. How could we shift to a shady place when just a ball could end the game? I closed my eyes and brought my mind to deep concentration to get a keener perception. And lo, it worked! I discerned why the match was dragging on. The match had to be played to the last ball of the last possible over of the day, because an over cut would mean the loss of a million rupees to the TV channel that had bought the broadcasting rights of the game. TV channel corporates were the new benefactors of the starving cricket stars, a role they had recently taken on from harassed bookies. I shared the insight with Shakeela and got a sardonic stare in return.

Lunch break came and we kept our eyes wide open for our son who might come out to have his grub. We had the consolation that he had purloined five hundred-rupee notes from Shakeela's wallet. He wouldn't have to starve. Lunchtime passed, and we continued to stand under the blazing sun, thirsty and hungry, longing for the ball that would clip Pakistan's tail and end our agony. That did not happen till the last possible ball of the day. I sought some relief from my frustration by watching the tension on the traffic policeman's face as the last ball was going to be bowled. He increased the volume of the transistor he was holding for my benefit. It was a nail-biting situation: If one of the Pakistani tail-enders hit the ball for two runs, he would win the game for his country and it would mean the end of the world; If he scored just one run, it would be an insipid end; And if he didn't score any run, it would be a magnificent victory for India and for the great game of uncertainties. Shakeela and I just wanted it to end, in whatever way.

The fatal last ball stayed glued to the Indian bowler's hand for about fifteen minutes, creating a killer suspense and allowing time for twenty-two more ads. When the bowler sent it down at last, the Pakistani batsman lofted it high over midwicket. The ball travelled high in the air to the boundary. It was going to be a six. But no! It wasn't! A gunshot hit the ball in the air right above the boundary line, splitting it into two. One half fell within the boundary and the other half outside of it. The policeman threw down his transistor. I picked it up. It was working. I followed the commentary intently. A scuffle to pin down the sharpshooter who downed the ball caused a big stampede. I could hear the sounds of a frightful pandemonium. I prayed to all the gods of all religions, and also to Baba, to safeguard my son.

The stadium started emptying out on to the roads, alerting Shakeela and me. Our eyes became as keen as the sharpshooter's. We would not miss anyone who resembled our son.

Just as the exiting crowd flowed like a rustled river in front of us, stranding vehicles, I saw Shakeela plunge in and wade through calling out, "Sunil! Sunil!" I looked in the direction she was calling but could not find our son. Shakeela strained her throat and struggled through the crowd for quite some distance and then halted, crying. I reached her by then. "He heard me and looked back," she said, weeping uncontrollably. "He disappeared between those cars. Why did he have to give me the slip?"

"It must have been someone who looked like him and not him," I consoled.

"No, it was him."

"There are so many veiled women around; how was he to know who among them you were?" I reasoned.

"Damn this veil!" she cursed. She took off the veil and flung it away to the road margin. "He's gone in that direction; Come, let's search for him."

We searched for him till midnight, in bus stands and railway stations, in restaurants and among urchins who slept on street-walks, but to no avail. We took comfort in the fact that nothing untoward had happened to him. Had I not put Shakeela back in the veil for my selfish ends, we would not have missed him outside the stadium. I was the culprit again… No, I wasn't the culprit. It all started with Murari killing my pets and getting rich.

We caught a taxi home after midnight. I saw someone in veil walk ahead of us as we entered our residential complex. The veiled woman was struggling up our stairs. Who could it be? We pussyfooted behind the woman at a distance. She stopped when she reached the door of our apartment and lay down in front of it. We went up to her. She was shivering.

"Who are you?" I asked.

The woman quaked.

"Get up!" Shakeela ordered, holding the woman by her hand.

The woman cried aloud. No, it wasn't a woman's voice, it

was our son crying! He was in Shakeela's old tattered veil, the one in which I had first met her. Shakeela gathered him up, removed the flap that covered his face and showered kisses on him while I unlocked the door. Shakeela rushed him to bed and pulled off the veil. He was burning and shivering with fever. We hugged him from either side and gave him warmth. He tried to say something, but he could not make himself clear through the clattering lips. I placed an ear close to his mouth and listened. Thanks to my keener perception, I was able to decipher what he was repeating in agony. He was asking, "Who won the match?"

I did not have a ready answer to the question. The suspense about the result of the match had shattered our son and caused the high temperature. I was sure the fever would subside if I could give him the answer to his question. The suspenseful ending of the friendly cricket test made me quake with anger.

"I do not know, dear," I said. "There'll be the one o'clock news in five minutes. We shall go and listen to it."

I gathered him and went to the living room. We lay on a sofa in front of the TV, hoping against hope that the Indian team had been declared winners. As expected, the first headline of the news was about the result of the match.

"The result of the friendly test match between India and Pakistan, which had a diabolic end today, has been referred to ICC for adjudication," the newsreader, a morose looking woman, read from our face. The detailed report on the subject quoted the umpire saying that he had taken the unprecedented decision because he was doing tight-rope-walking holding the two halves of the split ball in either hand for balancing and feared he would lose his balance and fall the moment he threw away one, declaring it the wrong piece. He was also constrained by the fact that the verdict might affect world peace, because his verdict either way could be interpreted as both just and unjust, and so, had the potential of becoming the flashpoint for World War III. He refused to go down in history as the man who had caused the war that would, in all probability, consume the world in a nuclear holocaust.

The Pakistani president's reaction was brought to us directly from his mouth. He appeared and filled the TV screen. "It is clear as daylight," he said, "that the umpire connived with the enemies of Pakistan and denied Allah's darling the victory she rightly deserved. None, except the blind, will have any doubt that if the ball had completed its trajectory, it would have hit some spectator in the stands. We request the ICC not to delay a second more in awarding the match to our country. I am constrained to add that Pakistan should not be held responsible for the sad consequences that a delayed or unjust verdict can cause. Let it be known to the entire world that we will not take an unjust verdict lying down. Vengeance shall be ours; we will repay even if it means we have to eat grass."

The Indian Prime Minister came on the screen immediately after. He intoned, "Our nation suffered the greatest treachery in history today when the umpire failed to award victory to us in the friendly test match between India and Pakistan. Our fielder was perfectly positioned to spring and catch the ball when a sharpshooter of Pakistan's ISI shot it in the air and it landed in two pieces. There again, justice was on our side, because the half that fell within the field had 'India' inscribed on it. We see a great conspiracy against our peace-loving nation in the refusal of the umpire to award us the victory we so rightly deserve. I appeal to my countrymen to remain calm and wait for ICC's verdict. I assure you that my government will react strongly if the ICC slaps an unjust verdict on us. (A pregnant pause.) And to impress on you that this government means business, I now declare a national emergency."

The emergency worked miracles not for my son or for cricket, but for the country, because from then onwards, the media brought home to us a new India where everything was rosy as in heaven. Within weeks agriculture production doubled, industrial output trebled, epidemics disappeared, life expectancy leaped from forty to seventy, child mortality fell from five hundred a thousand to twenty a thousand, the national integration index shot up from thirty to hundred, and the Prime Minister's age reduced from seventy to fifty.

The suspense about ICC's verdict prolonged indefinitely, and our son's fever followed suit. I took him to the best of doctors, but none could cure him. His fever was the physical symptom of a psychological problem, they opined. I thought as much – it was definitely linked to the disastrous cricket match. I shuddered to think of the tragic consequences that would follow if the verdict went against India. Our son could become delirious and go mad. He might even succumb to the fever.

The ICC seemed as reluctant as the umpire to give a verdict. They temporised on flimsy grounds.

Then, unexpectedly, the morning paper one day blazoned this headline: ICC AWARDS THE TEST TO INDIA. Our son's fever disappeared the moment he read it. He snatched the paper from me and devoured every word of the detailed report on the verdict. He then flung the paper at me and pranced about. He gave me a kiss, his mother a kiss and, for the first time in his life, his sister a kiss. He repeated the news report by heart to us a couple of times and then quietened.

Not a question had we yet asked him on his absconding – what he ate, where he slept etc. This I thought was the right time for it.

"Why did you abscond from home and give us so much

pain, son?"

"Because you gave me so much pain by not coming to take me to the match."

"I was so tied up with my work that the promise I made to you just didn't come to my mind. I was not in a position to come even if something did remind me of it. A cricket match is not as important as one's job, son. My job is a matter of our bread and butter."

"Cricket has forced the Prime Minister to declare a national emergency and you still hold that it is of small importance. When are you going to get your priorities right, papa?"

"I am working hard to get my priorities right, son. In fact, I am deeply involved in it now. Well, it's better we don't go further into such things. Tell me, how did you dodge the eyes of those who were searching for you?"

"I wore mummy's veil and sat near the ladies."

So, I was right after all. The boy whom Shakeela saw outside the stadium after the match got over was not our son. How could she have seen him if he was wearing a veil?

"And where did you spend your nights?"

"Near the ticket counter of the stadium. Long lines of people slept there in tandem every night to be the first to buy next day's tickets."

"Ladies too?"

"Yes, ladies too. Many of them wore veils. They bought

tickets and sold them at five times the rate. I too did the same with the money I had. I have earned enough money to buy tickets for the international matches that will be played here for the next ten years."

Our daughter came prancing and shouting, "April fools! April fools! You're all April fools!"

It was then that I realised that the day was the first of April. She showed us an insignificant box in an inside page of the paper, which clarified that the news item about the ICC verdict was an April Fools' Day hoax. We were back to square one. The ICC hadn't given its verdict. The National Chronicle had the tradition of playing the April Fools' Day hoax on its readers by carrying such sensational news. Our son started shivering. I felt his forehead. He was burning.

The suspense of ICC verdict continued with no signs of an early announcement emanating from any quarter. One only heard of high-level consultations aimed at formulating a verdict in which both India and Pakistan could claim victory. My hand continued to burn when I touched my son. I jettisoned allopathy and tried homeopathy, ayurveda, unani, naturopathy, pranic healing, magneto therapy and black magic, first in that order and then in six more combinations of order, all to no avail. It was then that a holy soul reminded me of something that I should have tried at the outset – faith healing. I was told of one Br Solomon, a member of a Catholic charismatic prayer group, who was a powerful faith healer. I learned that Shakeela and I would have to take the child to a retreat centre run by Bro Solomon in Kerala and attend a weeklong retreat there. There would be an ordinary faith healing session each evening and an extraordinary faith healing session in the evening of the last day of the retreat. All 'men of good will' would be healed of their ailments – physical, mental, spiritual, real, imaginary, past, present, future, and what not – in any one of the healing sessions. We went to attend the retreat, because it offered the only chance, other than ICC's verdict, for our son's cure. I was desperate to get back to Baba, but I couldn't till our son got well.

Bro Solomon was a saintly man of ordinary brains. It was a terrible disappointment in life that one day invested him with the supernatural power of healing. He read Dostoevsky's *Crime and Punishment* while he lazed away at home, waiting for an employment offer after securing a bachelor's degree in literature. He wrongly derived from the book this timely message: iIt isn't a serious crime for one to steal a few hundred thousand rupees for a good cause. He had a very good cause in hand. He was in love with a lovely girl whom he very much wanted to marry. The girl had put the condition to him that she would accept his offer of marriage only after he secured a government job. That was, and still is, the most difficult condition a girl could put to an Indian lover. For Solomon, it was an impossible condition, because he did not possess even a percentage of the market price a good government job commanded, five hundred thousand rupees or above. He had just enough money to attend a crash course on stealing, a novel self-employment venture another unemployed graduate had started. He passed the course with marks that his ordinary brains didn't really deserve.

One night he broke into the house of a rich relative who, he knew, had much cash with him. He successfully made away with a cash box containing six hundred thousand rupees. The Minister for Value Based Enterprises gave him a job as senior clerk in the district headquarters of his department for the money. The minister used the money only three months later, because he had older stock to use up. The man whom the minister gave the first pick of fifty thousand rupees returned the notes saying they were fake ones. It turned out that all the money Solomon gave the minister were counterfeit notes. The minister lost no time for punishing Solomon. His men, armed with iron rods, waylaid Solomon as he was walking home from office one evening and smashed his genuine head. He could later recall only the impact of the first blow that opened up a heavenly vision. He saw a blinding brilliant light through which a voice from heaven said, "Solomon, Solomon, rise and follow me. I'll make you a thief of souls."

And then the brightness of the light dimmed and he saw the face of Jesus. On the way, he lost his balance and he inadvertently touched a leprous beggar. The man's leprosy healed instantly. For three more days, every ailment of every woman, man and child he touched healed instantly. After that his healing power got restricted to the time he laid his hands on the participants of his soul-thieving retreats. The story of Bro Solomon reassured me that the small deceits I was guilty of would not stand in the way of my son getting a miraculous cure.

Bro Solomon was assisted by an impressive group of powerful voices to preach the retreat. They were women and men whose thunderous oration could put Hitler to shame. And they were people who could recite the Bible by heart, forward and backward. They quoted verses from the Bible as easily as Pandit Shingdi quoted astrological mantras. In the end of the day you got the feeling that you were hit hard on the head, and that was exactly the effect Solomon wanted. His own experience had convinced him that only a heady concussion could give the vision of God, that the Holy Spirit came with a bang.

One attractive part of the daily routine during the

retreat was 'giving testimonies'. It was the occasion when the participants made public confessions of the very serious sins they had committed. Bro Solomon and the preachers emphasized that those who showed the humility and courage to confess their sins in public would get, besides forgiveness, a great boon from the Holy Spirit. They would get the power to heal others by the laying of the hand. That was a very tempting offer. I wanted to go on to the podium and confess all the sins Mrs Murari had committed with me and get the power to heal my son. But a thought for the agony it would bring to Shakeela and Murari held me back. A middle-aged woman broke through such defences the devil put up and went up to the podium. "I beg of the merciful God and you my brethren to forgive me for I committed adultery with my neighbour Vakkachan last Easter night when my husband was away attending the midnight mass in our parish church," she boldly disclosed. The stunning confession was so chilling that electricity froze and the lights went off. I felt my son to see if the chilling effect had lessened his temperature. It hadn't.

It took more than an hour for electricity to defrost. When the lights came on again, Bro Solomon came to the mic and announced, "For those of you who have committed sins of adultery, it will be enough that they confess them to me in private when they come for counselling. They will also get the power to heal others. I prayed and got this concession for them from the Holy Spirit, because there is every chance that the light will go off too frequently and make it impossible for me to conduct the retreat otherwise."

The participants of the retreat had to attend counselling sessions which explored the psychological roots of their physical ailments. The counsellors included unemployed undergraduates, teachers, clerks, peons, nuns, seminarians, rubber tappers, butchers and illiterate housewives, who had obtained a doctorate in psychology by the power of the Holy Spirit, just the way Mary had conceived Jesus by the power of the Holy Spirit. The counsellor we were assigned to was a young priest. The first thing he did on seeing us was to bend down his head and pray silently for a few seconds. He then looked at us and said, "Black has always dominated your lives."

The blackening statement shocked us so much that we bowed our heads and prayed silently. I asked God to forgive him.

"Am I not right?" he asked, persisting with his black assessment of our family life.

We kept mum.

"It's a revelation the Holy Spirit has given me about you. It can't be wrong."

That made me reassess his statement... Yes, he had got the right inspiration from the Holy Spirit. The blackness of the solar eclipse, the blackness of the veil and blackness of my envious soul had dominated our lives. I thought it prudent to agree with the counsellor lest he should force me to agree by bringing out the black details about me in Shakeela's presence. I got convinced that the Holy Spirit had given him the clairvoyance to read every detail of my past.

"Yes, you're right," I said.

Shakeela gave me a baffled stare.

"One of you has had carnal relationship with a third person of the opposite sex," the Holy Spirit spoke through the counsellor.

It meant that the Holy Spirit had revealed my secret relationship with Mrs Murari also to the priest. He seemed intent on exposing me to Shakeela. What was I to do? I begged the Holy Spirit to spare me. And as I was searching for an urgent excuse to quit the counselling session, Shakeela spoke up.

"You are right," she said. "I was married to a sheikh for two months before we got married."

"I mentioned the two details about your past only to convince you that whatever I say is inspired by the Holy Spirit," the holy man said. "I shall not go deeper into your past. Now, tell me about the problem harrying you."

The relief I felt was so sudden and complete that I became breathless for a few seconds.

Shakeela explained the uncommon illness our son was suffering from and the untold agony it had caused us during the past many months. I supplemented her account with the details of the treatments we had tried. The counsellor listened to us with closed eyes and prayed for a while after we were done with our narrative.

He opened his eyes and looked at us with compassion.

"One of you fantasized a thrilling scene in a cricket match while you joined as man and woman at the moment of your son's conception. The boy's subconscious has been built over that thrilling cricket match scene. That's the reason for his addiction to cricket. And the worst effect of it is that his subconscious boils up whenever the suspense of a thrilling scene in a cricket match continues for more than a few minutes and causes high temperature."

That seemed a weird theory even if the Holy Spirit had inspired it. I liked cricket, but never so passionately as to fantasize it while having sex, especially with Shakeela. There was no question of Shakeela fantasizing a game that she considered to be a curse Satan had sent down to the world to spoil children's studies. In fact, it had often come in the way of our having sex, especially on days when there were day-night matches. And how could one believe the strange theory of the subconscious which claimed that fevers where caused by sexual fantasies? The theory didn't seem to have impressed Shakeela either. The priest divined from our incredulous stare that we were not convinced.

"The subconscious is a complicated thing," he explained.

"It holds a lot of seething secrets which can unexpectedly gush out and bring on the most frightful kind of mental or physical disease. Recently, I came upon a glaring case that can clearly bring home the point to you. A young mother came to me and complained that her child was not sucking. She was suffering great mental pain, because she thought her child was not accepting her as mother. She was suffering great physical pain, because her breasts were aching with clogged milk. She was writhing and entreating me for help. But how on earth could I help?"

If Shakeela weren't there, I would have told him how easily he could have helped the poor woman at least to relieve her of the physical pain. I decided I would give him some counselling on such practical matters after he had finished with his counselling.

"The cause of her problem lay in the subconscious," he explained. "She had conceived the child when she was not yet prepared to have a child. So she mentally rejected the child. That rejection registered in the child's subconscious and made it reject even life-giving milk."

I got the point: Behind the screen of Shakeela's dislike for cricket was her subconscious passion for the game. She must have fantasized cricket while she allowed me into her innermost self and conceived our son. She was merely pretending she disliked cricket while she was in truth an ardent fan of the game. She had been practicing duplicity just the way I had in many other things. She was no better than I.

"Is there a way we can do reparation for the mistakes of the past and be saved from the consequences?" I enquired of him. "For example, couldn't we have sex without fantasizing cricket a few times and undo the wrong?"

"There is always a way of atoning for even the gravest of sins. The penitence that the Holy Spirit inspires me to advise you is to forego sex till the next total solar eclipse."

I pretended to agree. Shakeela did not pretend to disagree.

Many people got miraculously cured during the healing session every evening. Stone-deaf grannies claimed they could hear. Thousands of people claimed that their headaches and stomach aches disappeared. People with impaired vision as well as people with normal vision got better vision. I did meet a couple of sceptics there who discounted the miracles saying that the four-thousand-five-hundred-watts speakers were so deafening to the normal ear that they could, in combination with thirty thousand straining throats, give the power of hearing even to stones. They even floated the outrageous theory that the intense sound deflated stomachs and cured stomach aches.

Irrefutable miracles usually occurred during the extraordinary healing session of the final day. The day started on an empty stomach, progressed on an empty stomach and ended on a stuffed stomach after receiving the miracles. The day would be bright if the monsoon wouldn't interfere, and the night would be dark immediately after darkness set in. That was the day of the week when lights would be off till the miracles happened. The extraordinary healing session would start with candle flames illuminating the Sacred Host in the monstrance and the transfigured countenance of Bro Solomon, who knelt gazing at the Lord in the Eucharist. It happened exactly so on the last day of our retreat, after a raving sermon by Bro Solomon, during which he broke a table into two by the power of his fists and tore his shirt into bits by the power of his claws. The electric organ played soul-stirring music and Bro Solomon twisted with pious emotions, his eyes beaming at the ascent and streaming at the dip. The music crept into him; socked his flesh, bones and morrow; gushed out as a tempestuous prayer out of his throat; the electric organ went into full volume; a hysteric mix of prayer and music exploded out of the four-thousand-and-five-hundred-watt speakers, pulverising the brain. Bro Solomon quaked with an ecstatic frenzy, like a Kali-possessed devotee, like a tantric healer; the frenzy engulfed me, like the mass frenzy of a houseful cricket stadium; "Halleluiah, Halleluiah, Halleluiah," I roared with the crowd;... The hi-fi speakers went suddenly silent; the frenzy dropped and Bro Solomon calmed down instantly and became dead still.

A power outage had deflated the healing session just as it was reaching its miracle-working climax. Power supply did not resume till next morning. No miracles took place that day. Our son did not get healed. Bro Solomon yelled some words of comfort for the disappointed participants through a bullhorn. "You must understand that we are not in the Old Testament times," he said, "when the prophet saw the Lord coming, not in thunder and lightning or in a storm, but in a cool breeze. Now, after Jesus' coming, the Holy Spirit comes and works his miracles only in dim lights and deafening clamour. It is to prepare the way for the Holy Spirit in modern times that God made man invent powerful sound systems. When they don't work, what miracles can we expect? This is not the first time that erratic power supply had deprived thousands of the miraculous cures they would have otherwise got. We will be able to find a lasting solution to the problem only if we buy a high-capacity generator which will cost around a hundred and fifty thousand rupees. I request you to help me with generous donations to buy the generator. Those of you who have not received the miracle you sought may come and try your luck again in the coming weeks. God bless you."

I did not donate any money to Bro Solomon, because, if worst came to worst and the ICC verdict was not forthcoming in a few days, I wanted to buy a generator and donate it to him, after mentioning it to Mr Murari. Shakeela and I returned home with our sick son, keeping the candle of hope burning in our hearts.

For a consolation, Bro Solomon's retreat chased Shakeela back into the veil, something that I very much wanted. She feared that our son's fever was a punishment from God for flinging the veil and abandoning it. She wore the veil at home also, as reparation.

Like a mirage, the ICC verdict held me back for quite some time from going back to Satsang Baba. Murari was back at his work during the day and back with Baba during the night. I was suffering a reversal of fortunes for which a glorious game like cricket should never have been the cause. Now that it was so, I fought hard to hold on to my faith in Baba and my pets.

My tenacity was soon rewarded. Five Muslim terrorists skyjacked an Air India flight carrying the Indian cricket team to London. The flight had three hundred passengers, mostly Britons of Indian origin and a nine-member crew. When Doordarshan broadcast the news at seven in the evening, the plane was in Kathmandu airport. The terrorists had freed all passengers other than the Indian team and the crew. They had threatened to kill the players one by one and finally blow up the plane if the ICC did not award the disputed India-Pakistan friendly test match to Pakistan within 24 hours. The terrorists claimed that they belonged to Allah's Prestige, a Jihadi group of Afghanistan that was desperately looking out for new Islamic causes for increasing the number of martyrs to fill the vast number of vacancies in heaven. Pakistani cricket was its latest Islamic cause.

The Prime Minister called an emergency meeting of the cabinet. The Indian government was inclined to order a storming of the plane, even it if meant the Indian players, who had caused the crisis by failing to take a tail-enders wicket during a whole day's play, would be dispatched to heaven along with the terrorists. But Ms Rambamba, the Minister for Heavenly Affairs, put her foot down and opposed any move that would give five more Muslims a chance for entry into heaven. She told the cabinet to be farsighted and see through the ISI's game plan to establish a Muslim majority in heaven.

The cabinet finally listed four options that could be adopted stage by stage while dealing with the skyjackers.

One: India to oppose any move to appease the skyjackers by awarding the match to Pakistan. India can accept nothing short of the unconditional surrender of the armed terrorists.

Two: India can make concession on the surrender of terrorists and allow them safe passage provided the ICC and Pakistan apologised to India.

Three: India can accept the blowing up of the plane along with the Indian players provided the terrorists accepted that they would not kill themselves and agreed to evacuate – this to satisfy Ms Rambamba who insisted they should not be allowed to use the crisis for gaining entry into heaven. A safe passage for the terrorists into Afghanistan could be arranged.

Four: If the terrorists insisted they would remain in the plane while blowing it up, India should allow the ICC to award the match to Pakistan.

The gunmen did not waste much time negotiating the first two options. They rejected them outright even as the ICC president mentioned them. More than three precious hours were wasted on the third option. The terrorists insisted that they would kill the players and embrace martyrdom if the match was not awarded to Pakistan. They refused to listen to the appeal of the negotiator that they could kill the players but should give a concession to India by foregoing martyrdom. Finally, India exercised its fourth option, minutes before the expiry of the deadline. The ICC awarded the disputed match to Pakistan and the crisis ended with the terrorists crossing over to Kashmir, which offered them another easy opportunity for martyrdom.

The Indian Prime Minister made the surrender a brave affair by going all the way to Kathmandu and garlanding the Indian players as they victoriously walked out of the plane. Shakeela and I joined a proud and grateful nation in thanking the valiant Prime Minister who, with a brilliant stroke of poetic imagination, saved the lives of India's ace cricket players and also upheld the nation's prestige by denying a chance to Muslim fundamentalists to become martyrs. Doordarshan broadcast a special message of the Prime Minister that evening. He explained the compelling circumstances that forced the government to take recourse in *ahimsa*, and concluded saying, "The one supreme consideration I had while negotiating the release of our cricket players was the integrity of our nation. The greatest achievements of our nation had followed the dictum 'good can come from evil'. The British conquered our subcontinent and looted it for more than three centuries, but a great good came out of the subjugation we suffered under them: They created the entity we now proudly call Mother India. Had not the British conquered us, this country would still have been divided into princely kingdoms that interminably fought with each other at the behest of foreign powers. Fissiparous forces are raising their heads once again seeking to divide our nation into pieces. A legacy of the British is helping us now to fight those forces. I am referring to the glorious game of cricket. The moment cricket falls apart, this nation will fall apart. Nothing holds this multiracial, multi-linguistic and multi-religious country together as cricket does. Nothing makes us feel as one as when India plays cricket with another country. Cricket alone binds our nation at this juncture when our enemies are instigating unpatriotic elements to take to secessionist activities. Indian cricket would have fallen apart if the lives of our players were not safeguarded. It is with the victorious feeling of having steered the nation clear of a great crisis that I exhort you to keep your heads high and shout with me 'Long live India, Long live Indian cricket.'

If one were to go by dry facts, the cure of our son's fever was the only tangible advantage India got out of the tragic episode.

Chapter - 7

Bumbum Raja Bumbum Rani

All was thus well with the nation, thanks to cricket. The Prime Minister took advantage of the countrywide feeling of well-being by going in for an early general election. For the first time, political parties sidelined film stars and favoured their cricket counterparts while allotting tickets. The one common promise that all parties made in their election manifesto was that, if elected to power, they would give a cricket ball and bat free every month to each household through ration shops. The money for it would be realised by selling off the huge buffer stock of grains the country had. There was a clear consensus among the political parties that the buffer stock had not succeeded in eradicating hunger, and cricket, on the other hand, would kill hunger and render the buffer stocks unnecessary. The Prime Minister's party swept the polls. The new cabinet had the distinction of having the world's first Minister for Cricket. For good measure, the Prime Minister appointed the Minister for Cricket his second-in-command.

All this didn't really hearten me. Cricket had disrupted my spiritual and physical union with Baba and put a question mark on the great leap my life was to make. I wanted to rush back to Baba, but Murari was there with him. Murari's absence from home didn't help me to have his wife more often either. Mrs Murari's acid-tongued mother ran away from home, chased away by her daughter-in-law's acid tongue and came to live with her daughter. The crone considered it her bounden duty to be with her daughter wherever she went unaccompanied by Murari. The more the daughter protested the chaperoning, the more the mother believed her darling needed it. The interfering hag succeeded in depriving my car of the scent of love for quite some time. In the whole of two months, only once did I get the opportunity to share the fullness of my love with Mrs Murari, and that happened in my house when Shakeela went with the children to her parents for a day to attend on her father after he suffered a near fatal heart attack and Mrs Murari's mother was laid down with dysentery. (Mrs Murari got so exasperated that she mixed some epsom salt in her mother's curry that morning.) I was having my next chance today. Shakeela had gone with the children to see her father, because he had had the second heart attack that morning and Mrs Murari had administered a second dose of epsom salt to her mother and got her hospitalised.

I had taken leave for a day and was waiting for Mrs Murari to steal into my apartment, but her father suddenly turned up and made up for her mother's absence. She had quietly rung up and told me that she would send her father away as soon as possible and come.

I had already gone through an hour of agonising wait and all I got was two more reminders by her that she would be with me within minutes. Minutes added up to hours and it was getting time for lunch and I realised Mrs Murari's father would not leave till he had lunch and a nap. There was also every possibility that he would bear up his daughter's hints to leave and wait to have a glimpse of the children after they returned from school.

The wait was telling on my nerves. I switched on the TV for relief. All the three channels I had access to were showing the same gods in almost the same attire, bellowing out the same dialogues to the same sort of people, in very much the same locations and settings, in identical stories of hardly dissimilar titles, rerunning mythological serials for the tenth, eleventh or twelfth time. The gods were being so overexposed on TV for commercial and political ends that they were becoming commonplace entertainers and losing their heavenly stature. They were depicted as little more than filmy heroes and heroines or fantastic creations like Superman and Mickey Mouse. I had often thought that it was high time that the king of the gods, Indra, took up the matter with the Minister for Information and Broadcasting. I for the first time thought cricket was a better choice. But even cricket wasn't available. I was going to play an audio cassette containing vintage Hindi numbers when I heard a knock at the door.

Here was my sweetheart at last!

I leaped at the door and opened it only to find a prudishly dressed woman in sari greeting me namaste. She was a stranger, a white woman, probably a European. I folded my hands in namaste and stood still till my disappointment dissipated and then welcomed her in.

"How are you, Shreeman?" the stranger asked, in a voice that sounded remotely familiar.

"I'm fine. How do you do?" I returned, feigning familiarity.

"Aren't your wife and children at home?" she asked.

"My father-in-law had a heart attack this morning," I answered, screwing up my brain to recall where I had met her. "They have gone to visit him."

"You haven't changed a bit since our last meeting here. The taste of the lunch your wife served then is there still on my tongue."

She had given me the right hint. She was the former

colleague whose nakedness had chased Shakeela back into the veil after I had coaxed her to discard it for the first time.

"Shakeela will be back tomorrow," I said. "You can savour the dishes again at your convenience. It will be our pleasure to entertain you."

"Thank you. I plan to stay for a month in this historic city. I hope to savour your wife's delicious food many times while I am here. I am researching for a doctoral thesis on the psychology of fashion. I am basing my thesis on the premise that nakedness is the beginning of fashion and the veil is the ultimate fashion. I thought you and your wife would be the ideal people I could interact with for an in-depth study of the psychology of the veil."

She was right, because no one else in the world would have lived out the psychology of the veil as much as we had. But what quixotic notion was it that made her consider the veil the ultimate fashion?

"I can well understand that nakedness is the beginning of fashion. It has to be so, because it is to cover nakedness that we wear clothes. But I had thought that the veil is the negation of fashion."

"You share the obscurantist notion a lot of people have about the veil. An unadulterated mind will easily understand that the veil is as much a statement of fashion as is nakedness. A man who can find a naked woman attractive will also find a woman in the veil equally attractive. If you get upset by the sight of a naked woman, you will also get equally upset by the sight of a veiled woman."

She was right there too. When I saw a veiled woman first, I had got as upset as I had been when I had seen her come out of the bath naked eight years ago. But now I was well at ease with the veil and even liked it. But would I be equally well at ease with her nakedness now? If only she would shed her dress and give me a chance to test?

"Okay, but why do you consider the veil the ultimate fashion?"

"Because beyond it is nakedness, from which it all started."

"When do you think film stars and fashion models will start wearing the veil?"

"At the space fashion is changing, we may not have to wait more than a decade."

"And after that you expect nakedness to become the fashion, don't you?"

"Exactly."

That gave me a good feeling, because I was young enough to live to those years when the days of Adam and Eve before the original sin would return. How I wished she gave me a foretaste of those days then and there!

"One thought about fashion that always comes to my mind is that we have every possible range of fashion from nakedness to the veil in the world always," I said. "Out of these, how does Paris or Milan choose one as the fashion of the year? Do they cast lots?"

"Now, that's a naïve question, Shreeman. Sorry for being so blunt; Fashion is not a mater of kismet. It is not such a simplistic concept. It is a very serious subject. In fact, today, nothing in the world is taken as seriously as fashion. The study of the progress of fashion is the study of the history, philosophy and psychology of the progress of man from the contentment of nakedness to the liberating protection of the veil through a relentless thirst for change."

That was too bewildering a statement. I accepted it for what it was and what it was not, in a bid to hide my bewilderment.

"Do you try out every fashion to research its psychology?"

"It becomes necessary in most cases."

"It means you are researching the psychology of the sari now, aren't you?"

"In the case of the sari, it is the other way about. I am wearing it because I have understood its psychology. In fact, I expect the sari to become the global fashion soon."

"That would be a great thing. So, that's how India, the sleeping tiger, will finally wake up and provide toilets to every household. But how did you arrive at such a conclusion?"

"Revealing dress and nakedness no more have the titillating charm they had before. Men are already complaining that they get deflated when they see a blatantly exposed female body. The preference now is for opening up covered secrets. That way the sari is the most titillating dress: It reveals enough to arouse and covers enough to provoke."

She was already arousing and provoking me more than I could stand. My eyes blinked to recall the breasts that dazed me once. It was as futile an effort as my waiting for Mrs Murari had been the whole morning. The double disappointment was driving me mad and propelling me to rip open her latest craze and see her nakedness, the thing that had once given me a blackout.

"I didn't really catch your point. Would you elaborate?"

"Many men have confessed to me that the exposed naval and the cleavage arouse them more than anything else can. And the cut of the blouse is so shapely that few things can provoke a man as much as the bust of a woman in sari does."

As she said that, the sari she wore slipped down from her bust and sanity slipped out of me. I pounced on her before she could draw the end of the sari up. She resisted. I pinned her down. She bit me. I threatened to kill her and gagged her mouth. Terrified, she submitted to my madness. I was tearing her open when I heard a knock at the door. I did not move. The knock thudded the door repeatedly, but I did not open. I knew it was Mrs Murari; Anyone else would ring the doorbell. The knock ceased and I plunged back into my carnal frenzy. I devoured the naked body that had made me tremble once. I felt no guilt. She was paying the price for having casually exposed her naked body to me eight years ago and I was letting her know that I had changed a lot from the gentleman and shy fool I was then.

The phone rang. I did not attend to it. I knew it was Mrs Murari. Some time had to pass before I could feel love for her. The phone went dead.

The guest arose and dressed up. Her blouse was torn to shreds at the hooks. She had a devastated look when she wore it. I came to my senses. What would become of me if she walked like that to a police station and complained that I had assaulted her? The consequences would be so terrible that I decided to take my life the moment she walked out. The stars of my pets alone could save me. They did. They prompted to me to fall at my victim's feet and beg pardon. I had become so selfish that I found it easy to fall at her feet and beg pardon for something for which I felt no compunction. "Please forgive me," I begged her, wetting her feet with my crocodile tears. "I don't know what came upon me and made me do this to you. Please do not tell about it to anyone. If you do, it will destroy my family and force me take my life. I shall pay you a good compensation."

"You life doesn't appear to be so precious a thing, Shreeman," she said, stone-faced. "The world can be a better place without people like you who turn to cowards in front of a woman when she comes naked and rape her when she comes decently dressed. I would have liked to scream and raise an alarm if by that I could have had the pleasure of seeing you quake to death on the halter before your neighbours came running. I am not going to do that, not because I fear you'll kill me before you hang, but because the thing you did to me has been a useful experience. It has given me some original insights into the psychology of the sari and the veil, which will make my thesis a bestseller. The millions I'll get and the fame my thesis will bring me will be compensation enough. Now, how am I to go out in this torn dress?"

I gave her one of Shakeela's blouses, but it was so small for her that she could not even insert her hands into it. I gave her a shawl and suggested she wrap herself with it. That gave her an idea. She picked up Shakeela's old veil which had fallen out while I was rummaging the wardrobe for the shawl. She slipped it on and walked out. I ran to my pets and thanked them for the salvation they had brought me.

I felt love for Mrs Murari after an hour. With her entering my life, love for me had become rarified to mean just sex. Armed with the definition, I followed the exhortation of St Augustine 'love and do whatever you like', the best way I could and became a worthy citizen of the 'civilised' world.

I rang up Mrs Murari. She disconnected the moment she heard my voice. I rang up again. She didn't pick up the phone. She was cut up, quite naturally. I felt terribly bad. I decided I would go to her and befriend her. But how was I to know her father had left? I had to meet her even if he hadn't. That would have been just wishful thinking had not Shakeela's veil come in handy again. I would wear it and fool the old man.

I put the veil on and walked in the direction of Mrs Murari's lap.

I heard a knock at my door even as I was nearing it. It was Mrs Murari no doubt. "Wait a minute," I shouted, and ran to the bedroom and took off the veil. I rushed back and opened the door. Yes, it was Mrs Murari. She didn't care to hear the excuses I had cooked up for not opening the door when she knocked twice earlier. She was that eager to have me.

As we were getting into the nitty-gritty of love-making, the doorbell rang. We lay silent. The doorbell rang again, now continuously for some time. Who could that be? Shakeela? We lay silent, waiting to see if the bell would ring again. It didn't. It might have been some door-to-door salesman. We made love, she ferociously and I half-heartedly.

She walked away satisfied and I followed her to the door to bolt it from inside. As soon as she opened the door and walked out, a woman-in-veil walked in. Mrs Murari bolted away to her apartment. I swooned.

When I came to my senses after a while, no one was to be

seen in the house. Shakeela had caught me red-handed and ran away from home! The woman was Shakeela no doubt. No other veiled woman would walk so freely into my house. She had rung the bell repeatedly and waited outside for quite some time. She would have plainly concluded that I had been making love with Mrs Murari. I was ruined!... No, the woman wasn't Shakeela. She wasn't supposed to come back the same day. How could she have turned up now when her father was in hospital, all set to leave for heaven? Besides, if it were her, the children would also have been there with her. I had unnecessarily got scared. But who was it then? The psychology-of-fashion researcher? I had treated her as the woman of the house and she could have taken the freedom to walk in. No. Why should she have returned wearing the veil after an hour? If only I had paid attention to the hands and legs of the woman in veil, I would have known who among the two she was. The woman had given me such a shock that my brain wasn't given time even to do that bit of a work. But why was I so upset when I had the means at hand to solve the mystery? I could ring up Shakeela at the hospital and find out if she were there. If she came on the phone, I could conclude that the woman who paralysed my brain was the fashion fanatic. It was as simple as that. I rang up Shakeela. My mother-in-law came on the phone. "Shakeela went out two hours ago to buy a medicine that is available only in a shop in the heart of the city," she told me. I hurriedly hung up. There was hardly any scope now to doubt that it was Shakeela who walked in as Mrs Murari walked out.

I could not take the help of Mrs Murari on my doubt. Where was the reason for her to doubt that the veiled woman was Shakeela? If I sought her help it would only serve the purpose of giving her doubts. There was just one more chance I could take, contact the woman I had raped. But I knew neither her phone number nor where she was put up. I didn't have the strength anymore to go in search of her as I had once searched for Mr Sreenat on a Total Solar Eclipse day years ago, setting in motion a stormy commotion in my life.

Even my pets wouldn't come to my help now. They wouldn't inspire a ploy to cover up things that they were witnesses to. And even if they did, no adroit ploy would ever convince anyone that a woman had gone into her neighbour's house when the man of the house was alone there for any other reason than to commit adultery.

Lying alone in my bed, my eyes kept vigil that night as my mind rankled and tossed me about on desperate choices. One moment, I decided I would confess everything to Shakeela and beg her pardon. She was the virtue that made my sins attractive. She was so good she couldn't but forgive me. The next moment my mind made a somersault and I imagined Shakeela refusing even to listen to me and slicing me with her tongue, razor-sharp with hurt. Moments later, I decided I would rush back to Baba's ashram even though Murari was there and get drunk on its brew of sin and salvation. Then again I decided I would elope with Mrs Murari to a strange land, carrying two bags full of Murari's money. There was a hitch there: I could coax or blackmail Mrs Murari into abandoning her husband and children, but I could never force myself to abandon my daughter and my son. I would rather kill myself than be separated from them. My mind returned to my first decision, to beg pardon of Shakeela. But it didn't stop there either. It reconsidered the other options. I thrashed over them the whole night without being able to make a final choice. Not until the clock chimed eight next morning and Shakeela and the children wished me 'Good Morning' did it quieten down.

Shakeela was glum, but not angry. Had she forgiven me on her own and come back?

"How is dad?" I asked, sitting on the bed.

"Couldn't you have visited him in the hospital and found out?"

"I wanted to, but some urgent work held me up in the office till late in the evening. I rang up to the hospital. You weren't there. Mummy attended the phone."

"She told me about it with tears. You didn't enquire

after dad, did you?"

I searched in vain for a credible answer.

"For what did you then ring me up?"

"I wanted to tell you I would be held up in my office the whole evening."

"Or was it to know if I would return yesterday itself?"

There it was; She was beginning to hit back. I kept mum.

"Dad is critically ill. I came only because the school is opening for the children today. I shall accompany them to the school and then go straight back to dad."

"I shall come with you. I'll ring up to my office and take a day's leave."

The emotion on her face did not change. She went about dressing up the children and packing the food she had bought from the restaurant in their carriers.

After the children left for school, we went to her dad in the hospital.

My father-in-law breathed his last before we reached the hospital. He was a good man. I know you won't take my word for it, because I am his son-in-law. Believe me; because I am only repeating the opinion of the hundreds of people who paid their homage to his mortal remains. Believe me also when I say that I was much saddened by his passing. He had done me a great service during his last days on earth: But for his illness, which made Shakeela absent herself from home many times, my intimacy with Mrs Murari would not have blossomed or flourished. It appeared as though his last mission on earth was to create a rival for his daughter in my heart. It also appeared as though, having got a hint that his daughter had come to know of it, he dared not face her again.

Deceitful as I was, I mourned his death deeply, and showed it. But I got no hint that I impressed Shakeela by doing so. Her father's death belied my hope that its pain would melt her rancour against me. She continued to smite me with a drawn face and tart remarks. She was in no mood to forgive. There was little hope of reconciliation.

This time around I had lost Shakeela forever. My children would also disown me. Left to myself, I would get sucked deeper and deeper into my deceitful self and collapse into a black hole, as dark and all consuming as the black veil.

Shakeela remained with her mother during the mourning period of forty days. I did not join the mourning, because I was convinced I wouldn't profit by it in any way. Instead, I did the only gainful thing I thought I could – love Mrs Murari desperately. Mrs Murari shared my anguish at having been caught red-handed by Shakeela. But impudence replaced anguish as the fear that Shakeela would shadow us then on made us reckless and unabashed. She stole into my apartment as often as she could, not bothering at all about Shakeela dropping in unexpectedly and catching us red-handed once again. We made the best of the forty days as though our lives would end with Shakeela returning home.

At what was supposed to be our last love-session during my father-in-law's mourning period, we spent quite some time discussing how we would face the situation when Shakeela returned.

"We shall just pretend innocence," I suggested. "Shakeela hasn't yet accused me of anything and I don't think she will ever do so. Whenever she caught me in wrongdoing, her strategy has been to rack me indirectly using it and wait for the chance I would offer her to blast me with it. This time around I shall make sure she doesn't get such a chance."

"You mean you will avoid me now on?"

"I will have to. Her eyes will hover over us all the time."

"But how could such fears keep you away from me, dear? Believe me; I cannot exist away from your warmth. Nothing can hold me back from you for long."

That was too fatal an attachment. It could lead to anything. It could even lead to her professing her love for me in Shakeela's presence in desperation if I made myself unavailable to her. I would get crushed between her and Shakeela, between lust and guilt. I had got so drunk on love that the hangover was going to torture me to death.

"We will have to be cautious at least till we find some way to dodge Shakeela," I cautioned.

"And if we don't find one?"

I had no answer and so kept mum, thinking. Then it hit me that there wasn't any need for me to have slumped into despair and become speechless when someone like Maharaj Trishankmurthy could easily show us a way out.

"I know a tantrist who can do the impossible," I said. "We can take his help. I have no doubt he will find some way to protect us from Shakeela's suspicious eyes. He once insulated me from her meddlesome nose."

"Then why wait?"

"I shall contact him on his mobile straightaway."

Trishankmurthy was lazing away at home when I contacted him. I explained my problem, giving every possible detail other than Mrs Murari's real name and identity. He said he would find a solution, but insisted that this time around no extra fee would substitute for the presence of the female involved while he extracted the solution from the gods. The fee he quoted of course included the extra amount he would have charged if Mrs Murari's presence were done away with. He suggested I could go to him immediately.

"He says he will solve our problem, but you'll have to accompany me to him," I said.

"What's his name?"

"Maharaj Trishankmurthy."

"He knows me. Murari used his service once when evil spirits invaded our factory in Bhopal and caused a major accident. He is a powerful tantrist, but he is sure to recognise me."

"He says he can work out the solution he has in mind only if both of us are present at the tantric rite he will conduct for it."

"We will have to think of not using his service then."

We had landed in a hopeless situation again. I took a last chance before I lifted the phone to tell Trishankmurthy that my paramour was not willing to come with me. I fed my pets and pleaded with them to show me a way. The parakeet chirped furiously, producing the same sound repeatedly. It was shouting what seemed to be a monosyllabic word. I strained my ears really hard, but to no avail. My cat tugged at my *lungi* and rushed to the bedroom when it got my attention. It pawed at the wardrobe. I pushed it away, because its paws were scratching the wardrobe. It returned and continued to paw at the wardrobe. I guessed it was asking me to open the wardrobe. I opened it. The cat sprang and pulled out a veil. Yes, the veil was the solution! Trishankmurthy would not recognise Mrs Murari if she wore the veil. My pets had become my redeemers once again.

We did not go to the tantrist; we asked him to come to my apartment instead. He agreed for double the fee. He trebled the fee when he saw my paramour in the veil – The mantras that could penetrate the veil were very costly, he reasoned.

He made us sit on my bed and he sat on the floor.

"I shall perform a rite whereby all the doubts your wife may have about your relationship with this woman will vanish," the tantrist said, facing me. "The rite will also focus your wife's intentions, mental vision and aim of life solely on your well-being. Whatever you do for your joy and pleasure will please her. She will no more get into silly doubts even if she happens to see this woman get in or come out of your house when you are alone. If you so desire, I shall also use mantras which will make your wife instantaneously enjoy the pleasure this woman will get when you make love with her, and vice versa."

Here, at last, was the secret whereby the rajas of old and sheikhs of the day kept their numerous wives contented. Oh, that I had learned this tantric wisdom much earlier!

"Use the mantras, Maharaj," I said, jumping at the offer. "How much extra will they cost?"

"I don't charge anything extra for those mantras. Lord Krishna directly revealed them to me and instructed that I recite them free as my contribution to promote family values in these times when men divorce wives every time they fall for other women. They can balance a man's devotion to his wife with his generosity towards other women and make divorces unnecessary."

Here was a hidden treasure of tantric heritage that could take the world by storm and straighten it. I was really excited, but I was at a loss to find out how Mrs Murari took it; She chose not to speak, and the veil hid her face. Then I saw her twiddle her thumbs and I took it as an indication that she too was excited.

Maharaja Trishankmurthy took out five dolls made of cloth from the handbag he had brought with him. One was of a male dressed like a groom and the other four were of females dressed like brides. He squatted the male doll at arms length and the four female dolls in a ring around it. He brought out a few more tantric objects like seashells, tiger nails, a monkey-skull, strands of human hair, flower petals, a brass handbell and a half-pint bottle filled with milk, and placed them between him and the dolls. He took out a brass plate and placed a few camphor pellets on it. He stared fiercely at the pellets. My eyes ached watching him stare. The pellets caught fire. Mrs Murari and I shuddered. He asked us to close our eyes. I closed my eyes. Did Mrs Murari close her eyes? I could only believe she did. He began chanting the mantras.

The tantrist chanted mantras for about twenty minutes before he asked us to open our eyes. The female dolls now stood in a single file, carrying the male doll on their heads. He asked Mrs Murari to lie on my lap and me to bend down and kiss her. He asked us to close our eyes again. I closed my eyes. I believed Mrs Murari too closed her eyes. He chanted mantras for about twenty more minutes and then asked us to open our eyes again. The dolls had all been stripped naked and were tied together in a bundle with the strands of hair, the male doll in the centre and the female dolls pressing against it on all sides.

Trishankmurthy closed his eyes and went into deep meditation for a short while. His lips then moved, reciting mantras silently. He ended the recitation with a yelp and placed a few camphor pellets on the brass plate. He stared at them as before, and they caught fire. He placed the dolls on the fire, and they blazed up. He stood up and vibrated like a plucked string, letting out a weird rumble and ringing the handbell, until the dolls were reduced to ashes by the camphor flame. He took some ash, mixed it in the milk and asked us both to drink the mix, sharing it equally. I drank first and offered the balance half to Mrs Murari. She took the bottle directly to her mouth, oblivious of the fact that it was covered by the veil. The stumble made Trishankmurthy giggle. Mrs Murari became nervous and her hand shivered as she negotiated the bottle towards her lips under the flap covering her face, straining not to uncover her face to the Maharaj's peering eyes. She paid the price for her inexperience with the veil. She fumbled and dropped the bottle, spilling its contents.

"Gosh!" the tantrist exclaimed, his face turning ashen. "It's a bad omen!"

I froze. Bad omens occurring during tantric rites foretell

terrible and irreversible tragedies.

"What does it forebode, Maharaj?" I stammered.

"Danger for her husband."

"What sort of danger?"

"A loss of equilibrium due to spilling of guarded secrets."

"Whose secrets, ours or her husband's?"

"Yours."

I would have had no reason to get upset if the spilt milk had foretold any danger to Murari other than the unsettling of his mental equilibrium. An unbalanced Murari would prove to be a worse torment than a suspicious Shakeela. To add insult to injury, the bad omen was threatening to bring to naught Trishankmurthy's efforts at locking up our secrets.

"Is there no remedy?"

"Not any that can cancel out the danger that the bad omen foretells. The only hope is an elaborate rite by which the danger can be transferred to someone else."

"How do you do that?"

"I would have to first transfer the dangerous effects of the bad omen to a sumptuous meal. Then I must serve the meal to an unsuspecting hungry beggar. It involves a rigorous rite, but the effects are guaranteed. The beggar will lose his mental equilibrium within forty-eight hours of his eating the meal."

"Will that prevent the spilling of secrets also?"

"No. But a simpler rite, which will insulate your secret

relationship from the effects of the bad omen, can be performed immediately."

"Will the rites cost much?"

"The cost of the rite that will transfer the ill effects of the omen from its intended victim to someone else is rather prohibitive, because I should observe a six-month gap between it and the next tantric rite. I will also have to perform special *poojas* for six months to cleanse the stains of cruelty that the rite will bring upon me. The rite that will safeguard your secret relationship from the bad effects of the omen is much cheaper. The two rites together will cost you two hundred thousand."

That was too big a sum to spend for safeguarding Murari's mental equilibrium even though it would hardly make any dent in the mountain of money his wife had put at my disposal. But there was a weightier reason than just the financial aspect of it for my deciding to settle for only the cheaper rite for the time being. The costlier rite would put Trishankmurthy out of action for six months, too risky a prospect when life was taking me fast through a knotty tangle of unpredictable events. I would require his services again any moment. I would rather wait and watch how harmful a deranged Murari would prove to be than lose Trishankmurthy's service for so long.

"I feel we should now go in for only the cheaper rite that will safeguard the secrecy of our relationship," I suggested.

"How much will it cost?"

"The two rites are irreversibly linked."

I had missed that point. I had no choice: It was either both or none.

"Okay, I agree to both. Is it possible to reverse the order and perform the second one first?"

"As a special case, that could be done."

"Please go ahead and perform it, Maharaj."

"You will be the main actors in the rite, and you may find it a little strenuous. So follow my instructions carefully. Any slip will have serious consequences. You will have to go through most of the rite blindfolded. Get me two rags or towels to blindfold you.

I took out two towels from the wardrobe and gave them to him.

"I shall go out of the room now," he continued. "You must take the leftover ash and smear each other's body with it. Take care to smear every part of the body with the ash. The holy ash will shield the sins you commit with your body from the outside world. Ring the handbell when you are over with it."

He went out of the room, closing the door behind him. We smeared each other with the ash, taking care not to miss any part of the body.

We dressed up and I rang the handbell.

The tantrist reappeared. He took out a fistful of camphor

pellets from his bag and placed them in the brass plate.

"I shall now blindfold you both," he explained. "By that the world shall get blindfolded whenever love brings you both together. I'll then conduct you around the flame a few times, forwards and backwards. You will continuously chant *'bumbum raja bumbum rani'* at the same pitch I will chant the mantra. After you have finished making the rounds around the flame, you will stand still and continue to chant the mantra at the top of your voice till I remove the blindfold. This part of the rite may take some time, but you must never pause chanting the mantra or remove the blindfold." He picked up the handbell and gave it to me. "You will ring the bell throughout while you chant the mantra."

He blindfolded us with the towels. I heard him strike the match. Within seconds, the smell of camphor hit my nostrils. He chanted *'bumbum raja bumbum rani'* in the pitch he normally chanted the other mantras. We chanted after him in the same pitch. I rang the bell. He held me by the arm and conducted me around the flame, forwards and backwards, forwards and backwards, backwards and forwards, forwards and backwards, backwards and forwards, forwards and backwards, forwards and backwards, backwards and forwards, forwards and backwards, the pitch of the chant increasing steadily, till I lost all sense of direction and I was chanting *'bumbum rani bumbum raja'* at the top of my voice. He made me stand still after I completed the sixteenth round.

But he continued to chant 'bumbum rani bumbum raja' at the top of his voice, and I chanted the mantra after him at the top of my voice. I rang the handbell in tune with my voice.

The rite was stretching more than I thought it would or I could stand. My throat and hands ached and began to sag. I feared the efficacy of the rite would suffer. He fell silent, giving me the hope that the rite was nearing its end. I called up all my reserved strength and made my throat and hands strain to their limits. He continued with the rite unbearably long, remaining silent all the while. The bell fell silent and my chant waned to a mumble. My stamina failed me. The rite would become ineffective! I turned blue with apprehension. In despair, I pulled down the towel that blindfolded me. Neither Trishankmurthy nor Mrs Murari was to be seen. There was foul play! I rushed out of the bedroom and searched for them. They were nowhere in the house. The main door was bolted from inside. They would not have gone out. How mysterious! Were they under my cot? I rushed back to my room. On entering it I heard Mrs Murari retch in the toilet.

She was bending down over the washbasin and Trishankmurthy was rubbing down her back. I rushed to her.

"It looks like the secret is already out," Trishankmurthy said. "Please get her urine tested."

Chapter - 8

Love In Paradise

Mrs Murari's urine created history, because, for the first time, the findings of three labs in the city concurred – my neighbour's wife was pregnant. Wasn't it indication enough that the child in her womb would rewrite history?

This is how I would have expected the scenario after the news of Mrs Murari's pregnancy to unfold :

> The results of the urine tests would devastate Mrs Murari. There were umpteen good reasons for her to be the mother of one more child, the most important of which was that late pregnancies always brought good luck. It would be especially so in her case. She had eight children. Even numbers are unlucky numbers, more so in the case of the

number of children one has. A ninth child would set right the numerology of her family. And then, the addition of a child wouldn't upset Murari at all. Mrs Murari had once confided to me that her husband had wanted her to bear and bring forth a child each time a national party split, giving birth to a new party, and it was she who had refused to oblige him. Murari's idea was to gift a son or daughter to each political party so that, whichever the party or coalition came to power, his business interests would be protected. Mrs Murari's objection was that it was beyond her capacity, nay, the capacity of any woman, to bring forth children at the rate conceited politicians were bringing forth new parties. Here was a belated compromise that fate had intervened and worked out. But for no reason would she be willing to accept the compromise and go through another pregnancy.

She would come to me drenched in tears and say, "This pregnancy will ruin me. I must get rid of it."

"I very well understand that a late pregnancy can be an irritant, but why does it upset you so much?" I would respond.

"Don't you get the seriousness of it, dear? Murari hasn't slept with me for the last three months and I am just three weeks pregnant."

"Then you're right; you must get it aborted."

"I need your help for that."

"How can I possibly help?"

"You must act as my husband. We shall fly to another city in the morning and fly back in the evening. The veil will camouflage me. I'll only have to spend a couple of hours in the hospital."

I would gladly give her the help she asked. A lady doctor would wash out the fruit of our love for a meagre two thousand .

But the unthinkable happened. Mrs Murari was in seventh heaven when she announced the result of the tests to me. She even congratulated me, presenting me a bouquet of yellow (my favourite colour) rosebuds. It was all so bizarre. Her infidelity would bulge out and confront Murari in weeks. Why was that not perturbing her at all? I strongly believed that I was the only other man in her life, and, for the same reason, was the father of the child that was growing in her womb. I liked the idea of having a millionaire child if it were possible to prevent the world from knowing that I was its father. But that was all just wishful thinking. Shakeela would be the first to question the legitimacy of Mrs Murari's bulging tummy. The veil could no more be a useful excuse. As long as my infidelity lay hidden from Shakeela, the veil was a useful justification for all my sly deeds, but not anymore. My infidelity was taking on flesh and would soon become a living testimony to Shakeela of it.

While these fears and more were scourging me,

Mrs Murari added insult to injury by audaciously exulting in the new fortune that had visited her.

On the day Shakeela and the children were to return, two days after the great secret was out, I was blinking at a file in my office and firming up a resolve to do some plain speaking with Mrs Murari about what we should do with the occupant of her womb when the intercom rang.

"Your wife has come to see you, sir," the receptionist informed me over the intercom.

I went dumb for a while. Shakeela had never before visited my office. The heavens must have fallen. The news of Mrs Murari's pregnancy must have already reached her. Had the spilt milk perhaps restored the uncanny powers of her nose? She was coming to attack! She might blow up and create a scene! I decided to take an emergency leave and go home with her.

"Ask her to wait at the reception," I instructed the receptionist. "I'm just coming."

I didn't have to make any effort to impress upon my superior that I needed to go home; He knew only too well that nothing but an emergency would have brought my veiled wife to the office. He allowed me to leave the office for the day. Luckily, he didn't embarrass me by asking what the emergency was.

"Come, let's go home," I told my wife, keeping my eyes off her out of fear and guilt, and walked out of the office.

She followed me into the car.

"What's the matter, honey?" I asked, getting into the car, "You could have rung up and asked me to come home."

"I want to spend some time with you alone," Mrs Murari crooned, towelling my face, her face still hidden under the veil. She was wearing a brand new veil. "Please take me to a hotel. I hope I have not upset you by coming to your office. I know I should have rung up and come. That's what I should have done. But your love is making me forget proprieties. It'll not be easy for me to get you after Shakeela and your children return this evening. I came to request you to take a half-day leave and take me to a hotel. I feared you would not oblige if I made the request over phone."

"That's okay," I intoned, swallowing the abashment of being cheated by the veil.

"Now I know you too were eagerly wanting to get me alone. Thank you, sweetheart."

"You bought a new veil, didn't you?"

"I bought a new one, because I may have to use the veil more often now on."

"Please give me a hint when you come to me in the veil next time. I actually mistook you for Shakeela."

"Is that why you came away promptly?" There was sadness in her tone.

"No, not that. It was why I looked a little upset."

The explanation seemed to satisfy her, as if she was

waiting for an excuse to get blithe again.

I drove to Hotel Hideout International. She kept towelling my face as I continued to sweat profusely, struggling not to allow the natural fervour of her love to weaken my resolve to have a serious talk with her.

ꕥꕥ

"Please let us get the child aborted," I entreated her as her lips invaded my face. "It will ruin us if it is allowed to be born."

"I will not get it aborted," she said, her face glowing to match the elegance of Hotel Hideout International's luxury room. "It's the fruit of our love. It's the greatest thing to have happened to me in life."

"But we will get exposed if the child is allowed to be born. I will die rather than face such a situation."

"I want to be mother of your child and live."

"You are courting hell."

"You, me and our child together can only mean heaven for me. I am standing at the threshold of that heaven. Hold my hand and lead me into it. Let's elope."

"Elope? How can we?"

"Why can't we?'

We spent quite some time discussing answers to those questions. I appealed to her to be practical and realistic, but she was drunk on love and refused to be anything but romantic. She had her reasons for it. Murari and she were first cousins. They were married in their early teens. Marriage was for her no more than a passing from one form of relationship to another form of it with the same man. The romantic passion that she was getting from our relationship was alien to it. Murari had been a good cousin and a good husband, but never the lover that I was. It was with me that she had the real experience of loving a non-relative and being sought after by a non-relative. I came to realise that there was no use talking sense to a woman who was having her first crush at the age of forty-three. And then, Murari had eloped with Mammon and practically left her to herself. She was willing to discuss only one choice – elope or embrace death together.

My deceits had come home to roost. If I eloped, guilt would tighten like a noose and choke me to death. The better choice was death.

We agreed to embrace death together – after five days.

I stayed away from office and spent the next five days with Shakeela and the children at home. Shakeela was her old good self when she returned. She behaved as if she didn't mind my relationship with Mrs Murari at all. The solar eclipse that brought us together was going to take its toll after all. How much she had loved me and what a traitor I had turned out to be! She once shed the veil that was as much a part of her as her skin, mentally bearing all the pain of being skinned alive, for my sake. In return, how cleverly I had used the veil to deceive her! I had used the black thing so often that it had become my protection and my refuge. The world would soon know what a treacherous husband I was to her when Mrs Murari and I would be found lying dead in the luxury car I had bought with Murari's money.

The children clung to me all the time as though they had missed the nectar of my love for too long. There was a five-day cricket test match between India and Sri Lanka going on. I permitted my son to skip school for the five days. We enjoyed the match thoroughly; The Indian players were in great form. Shakeela, the children and I together were so beautiful a heaven that heaven was the price I was going to pay for mortgaging my soul to envy.

ꕥꕥ

The appointed hour was at hand. Mrs Murari would be waiting for me at the entrance of Wild Life, a downtown shopping complex. She would be wearing a veil. Shakeela was in the kitchen, preparing my favourite fish curry for supper, and the children were watching the final day's play of the India-Sri Lanka cricket test match on TV. I fed my cat milk and my parakeet grains. I opened the cage of the parakeet and watched it flap off out of sight.

My heart murmured a silent goodbye to my heaven.

When I stepped out of it, I had the satisfaction that I had kept two million of Murari's money in fixed deposits in Shakeela's name. I walked fast to my car. Mrs Murari would expect me at half-past-five sharp. I would have to halt on the way to buy two small bottles of poison and two gold goblets and reach her in thirty minutes. (It was Mrs Murari's idea that we should seal our golden relationship by drinking poison from gold goblets.)

I heard a lady say 'hello' as I was getting into my car after buying the gold goblets. I turned to her. She was the fashion fanatic.

"You really frightened me that day," she said. "I returned to get your phone number. You swooned seeing me. I scooted out fearing you had dropped dead."

"So it was you?"

"I guessed you had mistaken me for your wife. You're a great one: Made it with your neighbour so shortly after you made it with me. I travel a lot and have made it with a lot of men, but never with a stud like you."

"I thought I had wronged you. Happy to know you have taken it well."

"And I must tell you that your swooning helped me complete my research into the psychology of the veil, giving it a veritable U-turn. You gave me the veil to cover the crime you had committed against me and within an hour you passed out seeing me in the veil. I now see an apocalyptic sign in the veil. When the veil becomes the fashion, we shall know that the end is near. This dramatic twist will make my thesis the hottest publishing product yet."

I hardly heard what she said, because I was engrossed in the revelation that it was she and not Shakeela whom I had seen in the veil when I opened the entrance door of my house for Mrs Murari to slip out. So, Shakeela had no reasons to doubt me, and she hadn't really doubted me. (The gravity of her silence was the gravity of the grief of her bereavement.) The revelation was making me take a U-turn.

"Thank you," I said, and hurried into my car.

I sped away.

Mrs Murari had just reached the entrance of Wild Life when I pulled up my car beside her. She leaped in. I hastened, because I had to reach a deserted stretch of National Highway 001 before doubts and prevarication restrained me from putting my interests first.

Mrs Murari took off the veil. Draped in a rich sari, wearing stunning jewellery, elegantly made up, gazing with innocent and radiant eyes, and splashing a winning smile, she was a new ravishing beauty. I admired her for a moment before pressing the accelerator.

"You look quite an eyeful," I said. "You didn't look so even at your silver wedding anniversary."

"This is the greatest occasion in my life. I am flying on a honeymoon trip with you to heaven. You will feel small if I look ugly in the company of angels."

"The angels are going to feel small in your presence."

"The credit is yours, darling. Your love has worked the transfiguration." She pecked my cheek.

I braked the car behind a long queue of vehicles at a traffic signal. My eyes devoured her. Her beauty rushed through my blood and surged me. My head dipped into her bosom. I didn't see the traffic move ahead till the deafening horns of stranded vehicles pulled my head up.

"I shall put on the veil if I am disturbing you too much," she said, flashing a mischievous smile.

"Please don't, the veil will block your glow. A little while and I will lose it forever. Up in heaven, some archangel may snatch you from me."

"I have become so much a part of you that no archangel will be able to separate us. We have melted in the heat of love. Death shall soon join us and make us one. In heaven, we shall have no separate existence."

She rested her head on my lap. I pressed the accelerator full and made my car skim the highway.

"No fragrance can ever smell as sweet as your sweat, darling," she murmured. "No flesh can ever warm up a dying soul as yours does."

I negotiated a herd of frolicky buffaloes by slowing down.

"No breath can ever give life as yours does, darling." Her fingers groped their way among the bush of my chest to my thumping heart. "No heart can ever resuscitate another as yours did."

A calf pranced across my path; I braked my car.

"No mouth can ever sing the song of the heart as yours does, darling," Her fingers played on my lips. "No eyes can ever radiate love as yours do."

The sun turned crimson and sank below the highway straight ahead of me. Darkness slipped over the countryside like a veil. I pulled over and made love with her under the cover of darkness.

Fireflies swarmed the car and twinkled, bringing heaven close. I took out the gold goblets and gave them to Mrs Murari. She held them as reverently as a priest would a chalice. I opened the two bottles of poison and emptied their contents into the goblets. She gave me one of the goblets. We kissed each other for one last time. We raised the goblets in unison to our mouths. She turned her face away and drank the poison. She didn't turn back again. I flung out of the car and slammed the door shut. I threw my goblet along with the poison into the thorny hedge nearby, walked away to a distance and waited, giving her ample time to convulse and die.

I opened the door of my car and had just a glance at her under the courtesy light. Her body was limp. She lay prone on the seat. There was a wide trench at the roadside, formed long ago along much of the highway by excavating soil to build the road. The moon had by now just crested the horizon and made everything faintly visible. I scanned the highway, which stretched like a straight line to either side. No vehicles were approaching. I removed the jewellery from her and stuffed them into my pockets. I dragged her body out. It still felt warm. I rolled it into the trench. It lay half-immersed in water, face up. Her lips were shut, but there was the smile of love on them. Her eyes were open, and there was the sheen of innocence in them.

I picked up the veil and threw it away into the trench. It spread out and fell on her body, covering her face and upper half. The world would not know of Mrs Murari again till the stench of her body harried it. I hurried into my car and sped cityward.

Fireflies had swarmed into my car when I opened its door to drag Mrs Murari's body out. They now swarmed about me like sparks from hell and singed the exposed parts of my body. My face streamed with perspiration. My vision got blurred. I checked the AC. It was working. I wiped my face and drove like mad.

The skyglow above the city was double bright. As I approached the city, I realised that it had burst into a mad celebration. Revelling crowds filled the streets, bursting crackers and dancing to the beat of drums. 'What could be the reason for the mad rejoicing?' I could not stop the car to enquire. I made it crawl forward.

The city was gaffawing like a monster and getting on my nerves. I was ready to explode at the least provocation, when a lone reveller blocked my way. He was holding aloft a bottle and swaying. "Have a drink, sir," he drawled.

"Get out of my way!" I shouted.

"Don't bristle at me, sir. I'm offering you a drink," he said, sporting a befriending smile, which suddenly cooled me.

"This is scotch, sir," he boasted, coming close and offering the bottle. "Gulp it down neat. The gods have safeguarded our nation's prestige at last. It's after thirty-one years that we have got a real occasion to celebrate."

I had no idea what he meant, but the scotch whisky appealed to me as a welcome bracer. I accepted the bottle. It was a quarter full.

"Thank you, rich man, for accepting my drink," he said. "You can have the whole of it. I'll buy another bottle. I'll drink and make merry the whole night... I'll buy a bottle for every six Arjun hit over the heads of forty thousand Sri Lankans to give India its first test victory abroad in thirty-one years. That last six Arjun hit made our miserable lives worth living, sir. I don't see India winning another test abroad in my lifetime."

Chapter - 9

At The Threshold Of Hell

Thanks to cricket, for the first time after India's 'tryst with destiny', the whole nation had exploded into a nightlong mad celebration. Sounds of revelry pulverised my scotch driven brain and the control I had over my car loosened to the bare minimum, raising its speed to the maximum. Luckily for me, I was taken for a drunken reveller from whose path anyone who valued his life must flee and I reached home in one piece, but the car came to a perfect halt only after it hit against the rear wall of the car park, shattering its eyes and shaking me back into my senses. Luckily for me again, the boom of fireworks drowned out the sound of the crash.

I sat in the car, thinking. 'Oh my God, what have I

done! What will be the consequences? How will I face them? Someone will discover Mrs Murari's body and report to the police. They will search for the murderer. Have I left any clue? Not any I can think of... But what if the postmortem reveals a man has lain with her! It will then become a case of rape and murder. Have I left anything there which would lead the police dogs to me? I haven't... No, I have! The gold goblets and the empty poison bottle!' I searched in the car and found the goblet used by Mrs Murari and the empty poison bottle lying on the back seat. I suddenly recalled I had thrown away the goblet I used. 'The game is up for me. The goblet will lead me to the gallows... Perhaps, no. Anyone who finds a gold goblet will pocket it, especially if he is a police officer. Even in death, Mrs Murari has become my saviour: But for her insistence, I wouldn't have thought of buying gold goblets.' I picked up the gold goblet and the poison bottle from the backseat and stuffed them also into my pockets. 'Where can I safely hide them and Mrs Murari's jewellery? Rush to Baba's ashram early in the morning? There surely cannot be a better place to hide after committing a crime. But taking refuge in Baba's ashram may not be the wisest thing to do: If I am suddenly found missing from home tomorrow, it could raise suspicion about me. Where else? I need to confess my crime to someone and find some relief and guidance. But where in the world can I find someone I could trust for that?... Yes, there's someone

– Maharaj Trishankmurthy. In exchange for Mrs Murari's gem studded jewellery and the gold goblet, I'll ask him to perform a rite that will protect me from all suspicions from all quarters. The gifts are of more worth than the price of the costliest rite imaginable. Yes, come dawn and I shall rush to Trishankmurthy at whichever place I can find him... But, just now, how will I face Shakeela and the children? What explanation will I give them for getting drunk and hitting my car against the wall? I shall put the blame on cricket: I got carried away by the nation's mood.'

My bladder started aching and I rushed up the stairs leading to my apartment.

The moment my son opened the door, I pushed him aside and made a dash for the toilet. As my bladder began emptying, anxious questions began filling my brain again. 'My pockets can catch Shakeela's attention as soon as I walk out. How will I keep Mrs Murari's jewellery and the other contents of my bulgy pockets away from Shakeela's eyes till dawn breaks? In the toilet of course. There are only two possible places in it – my toilet kit bag or the waste basket in the corner there... The waste basket is the better option.' I took out the precious pieces from my pockets and hid them in the half-filled waste basket.

Shakeela was waiting at the toilet door as I opened it.

"What a great a victory it was!" I exclaimed, holding Shakeela tight.

"Indeed, darling," she crooned. "May Allah be praised for this blessed day! Our son is in the seventh heaven. I haven't ever seen him so happy. And I wonder if another such day will come in our life again. Let's celebrate. I've prepared a grand dinner."

We walked to the hall, my right hand around her waist and her head on my shoulder.

"The *sharbat* you drank smells very different," she says, sniffing my mouth. "Where did you get it?"

"A reveller gave it when I got caught in a traffic snarl," I replied. "It tasted pungent and I felt tipsy after drinking it. I was in a kind of seventh heaven till the car hit against the rear wall of the car park and stopped."

"Yah Allah!" She ran her eyes all over me. "Did you get hurt?"

"I'm perfectly okay. The car had almost come to a halt when it hit the wall. Only the headlights got damaged."

"They might have mixed ganja in the *sharbat*. Thank Allah you came home safe."

When we emerged into the hall, our son was jumping on the sofa, watching the all night non-stop replay of Arjun's six that had sent the nation into seventh heaven. I stood beside him and waited eagerly for my first glimpse of the shot. As the bowler was sending down the ball, 'BREAKING NEWS' flashed on the TV screen. "Here is a breaking news," a lady appeared and announced. "In an emergency cabinet meet called at the stroke of midnight hour exclusively for the purpose, the union cabinet has decided to confer the Bharat Ratna on Arjun... " My son leaped on to my back shouting, "Hurray!" I lost my balance and fell, hitting my head against a teepoy. I passed out.

When I regained consciousness, I found myself lying on a hospital bed, flanked by Shakeela and a nurse. The first thing that came to my mind was the total solar eclipse, the effect of which had brought me unconscious to a hospital bed nine years back. There was a big difference this time around though: Instead of yelling with fear, Shakeela quaked with joy on seeing me open my eyes and motion for water with my hand. The nurse quickly produced a glass of water and handed it over to Shakeela, who raised my head with one hand and fed me water with the other. I saw the nurse run out of the room shouting, "He has regained consciousness!" Not until Shakeela had lavished kisses on my cheeks and wet them with tears of joy did I come out of the delusional feeling that it was yet another total solar eclipse day.

"How long have I been here?" I asked, as I saw a doctor and a couple of nurses walk into the room.

"Thirteen days," Shakeela answered.

"Can you remember what brought you here?" the doctor asked, gifting me the broadest smile I had ever seen.

I groped for a while, and then said, "Arjun's six."

"Over twelve thousand people got injured in accidents

and around two thousand went into coma in one night because of it," he said. "You're the only lucky one yet to come to. Thank your lucky stars."

"Thanks be to Allah, the Merciful!" Shakeela corrected, holding her hands in a pious gesture.

Mrs Murari and her fabulous jewellery kept coming as singing flashes even as a steady stream of visitors kept me back from dwelling on them. My children came rushing from their school within minutes of my regaining consciousness. Getting my old self back made my son so hysterically happy that he declared in the presence of a roomful of visitors that he would never again watch cricket on TV. When my daughter sought a clarification on whether he would watch the game in stadiums, he said he left that to my sweet discretion. What capacity for love at so young an age! I felt so hysterically happy about his resolve that I would have passed out once again had not Mrs Murari hit my brain at the nick of time.

That night, Shakeela had a good sleep after thirteen days and I lay awake, haunted by Mrs Murari. The anxiousness to know about the aftermath of her death was banging at my brain. All my close acquaintances except Murari had visited me after I regained consciousness. I could have asked Shakeela why he and his family hadn't turned up, but I dared not, fearing it might expose me. But why didn't Shakeela tell me anything about her? Was she waiting for me to fully recover before giving the shocking news? What had happened to Mrs Murari's jewellery and the gold goblets? Were they still lying undisturbed there in the waste basket? Or would my daughter or some kindly relative, who stayed at my home and looked after the children in Shakeela's absence, have handed them over to the garbage collector along with the waste? I tried in vain to get sleep by taking comfort in the thought that, if Mrs Murari's body had been recovered and the needle of suspicion for her death had in any way turned towards me, I wouldn't have been so euphorically welcomed back to conscious life. How I wished someone would speak to me about Mrs Murari as soon as the day would break!

I stayed four more days in the hospital, sleeplessly awaiting the name of Mrs Murari to fall from someone's lips, which finally happened in the late evening of the fourth day when I was alone with Shakeela, a couple of hours after the doctor let it known to us that I would be discharged from hospital on the following day.

"Now that you have fully recovered, I would like to break a sad piece of news that will be awaiting you at home," Shakeela said, in an apologetic tone. "Mrs Murari met with a tragic death."

"What?" I exploded. "Some accident?"

"It looks like murder. Her body was found in a trench fifty kilometres away on highway 001. The police have arrested a garbage collector who was found in possession of her jewellery. The police claim he has confessed to the murder."

I pretended shell-shocked, but the superhuman effort I made to squeeze out a tear was defeated by the relief I felt at not having become a suspect for the murder.

"Did he kidnap and kill her?" I asked, emerging out of the pretended shock.

"That's what the police say. He raped and murdered her. But I suspect there is something more to it."

'Has her nose regained the power to smell secrets!... No. If she has, she would have discovered that I was the murderer.'

"What do you mean?"

"He must have been having an illicit relationship with her," Shakeela explained. "She used to complain often to me how lonely she felt after Mr Murari started staying away from home in Satsang Baba's ashram. Then she suddenly stopped the whining some three months ago. Driven to desperation, she must have fallen to overtures made by the garbage collector, who I can vouch is a very indecent man."

"Has he made such overtures to you?"

"Not to me, but Mrs Murari did tell me once that she

didn't like the way he stared at her when she handed over the garbage to him one day."

"If you had told me about it, I would have taken some action to stop him from collecting garbage from our complex," I said.

"I do feel a bit guilty on that count," she confessed. "But she never again mentioned he repeated that behaviour. Besides, we women imagine such things sometimes."

"How can you then, just on that count, conclude she had an illicit relationship?"

"My suspicion is based on something more serious," she said. "Her body was found covered with a veil. It must have been the same veil I found missing from our wardrobe when I returned home after father's death. She must have stolen it while I was away."

I kept mum, thinking how Shakeela, of all people, could accuse a dead woman of theft. Had she nurtured some dislike for Mrs Murari?

"She was using the veil to cheat on her husband," she continued. "Even if it were not my veil that she used, she has sinned against the holy veil by using one to commit adultery. I'm greatly saddened by her tragic death, but am wont to think it is Allah's punishment for defiling the heavenly garment."

I felt so sad for her that she was saddened more by the abuse of the veil than the death of a neighbour that I wanted to tell her, 'Now, I can understand your fondness for the veil, but, for Allah's sake, don't elevate it to such divine level,' but I chose not to. Instead, I asked, "Do angels in heaven wear the veil?"

"Of course they do," pat came the reply.

"How did the man kill her? By strangling?"

"No. She consumed poison. The police say he tricked her into taking a drink laced with poison. And that strengthens my suspicion that she was having an affair with him. When the sheen of the relationship faded out, he must have thought of getting rich by killing her and getting away with the gem studded jewellery. They are worth at least ten million, you know."

"How could a man be so cruel!... How has Murari taken the tragedy?"

"The poor man is devastated," Shakeela said. "He's not able to face people. A glum shake of head or nod is all that you can get out of him. And yet, he was elated when he heard you regained consciousness."

"He is so good a man," I reciprocated. "Why does Allah punish good people like this?"

"It's not enough for men to be good; They must also have faithful wives if misfortune is not to befall them."

A knock at the door. A nurse opened the door and entered, holding medicines in a tray.

As the nurse gave an assortment of seven tablets and

a glass of water and I swallowed the tablets one at a time, Shakeela went through a pile of newspapers and pulled out a sheet. As soon as I was done with the tablets, she gave me the sheet. There was in it a half-page exhaustive report on Mrs Murari's murder. The paper also gave a photo of the garbage collector. He was the same bearded man who regularly showed up every morning at our entrance to collect garbage. According to the report, the murderer was tipped off by a jeweller to whom he had taken the ornaments. Although he denied any role in the crime during five days of questioning, he finally broke down and confessed to the crime. The description of the modus operandi of the crime appeared to me as both fascinating and bizarre. He had set his eyes on the jewellery many months back, after seeing Mrs Murari come out wearing them many times. He slowly won Mrs Murari's confidence and goodwill by going on errands for her in the three-wheeler he ran as a taxi after his two-hour garbage picking rounds, charging her just the meter fare. He then waited for a convenient day when he could kidnap and murder her as she came out wearing the ornaments. The final day of the test match between India and Sri Lanka filled the slot perfectly. She madly wanted to watch the last day's match, but her driver fell sick. Determined not to miss the match of a lifetime, she asked the garbage collector to take her in his three-wheeler to the stadium. When she emerged from the stadium after the test match, he offered her a bottle of poison laced coke. As the city lost itself in a mad rejoicing, he sped off to highway 001 with the dying Mrs Murari. After he was satisfied that she was dead, he threw her body into the trench and covered it with the veil he always kept in the three-wheeler for secretly ferrying call girls and prostitutes to their clients.

A rather credible story, no doubt, but why did the man own up a crime he had not committed? Well, the police must have found it hard to get any other clue than the jewellery to solve the mystery of the murder and so tortured him into admitting to the crime. Quite the order of the day.

'I find you guilty on three counts: one, killing a woman who loved you more than she did anyone else or even her own life; two, an innocent garbage collector and his family are going to suffer the consequences of a horrible crime you committed; and three, you have desecrated the holy veil.' My conscience kept repeating throughout the night, very much like the replay of Arjun's six on TV on the night of my fateful fall. And in an effort to ward off the accusation, I dwelt on each of them.

'Yes, I am guilty of killing a woman who loved me as immensely and selflessly as a woman possibly can; But it was my sincere intention to embrace death together with her. A chance meeting with the veil-psychologist was responsible for the twist of fate that gave me a new life. We are all playthings in the hands of fate. Need I be held guilty for the crime fate has wrought? And even if I am presumed guilty, I am going through the punishment for it by wearing a crown of guilt which is lacerating my head from all sides. For her sincere love, fate has rewarded Mrs Murari with escape from an agonising guilt-ridden life. This new life and this regaining of consciousness are the punishment I got for cheating two women who loved me dearly, Shakeela and Mrs Murari. Buying another gold goblet and fulfilling the final promise I made to Mrs Murari seems to be the only way of escape from it.

'As for the garbage collector, he has brought the fate upon himself. If he were a good and honest man, he should have handed over the ornaments to the police. Why blame me for someone paying the price of his avarice and dishonesty? But is it right to expect such honesty from a poor garbage collector when avarice has led Murari and me along the path to ruin? I feel sympathy for him for not possessing a nobler soul than ours. I only hope he gets a good lawyer who can prove his innocence to the court as far as Mrs Murari's death is concerned. When a flamboyant lawyer can easily impress the court with the most illogical argument and win a not-guilty verdict for his murderer client, the garbage collector stands a good chance of acquittal since he is innocent. Look at the Oscar Pistorius trial. So many months of investigation, so many hours of court hearing involving legal luminaries and so many days of judicial deliberation produced so silly a not-guilty-of-murder verdict. Common sense tells you that the moment Pistorius heard someone's noise in the adjacent toilet, he should have normally thought that it was his bedfellow, the girlfriend, who was in the toilet. And if he did at all suspect an intruder, common sense says he should have immediately checked if his girlfriend was there sleeping beside him. How could his eyes have not fallen on Reeva, who was supposedly sleeping on the window side, as he went about drawing the curtain, opening the door leading to the balcony, taking a pedestal fan from there to the bedroom and drawing back the curtains? If the room had become pitch dark after he drew back the curtains, he had to do no more than stretch out his hand and grope to find out if she indeed was in the bed. If he didn't find her there, he should have normally concluded that she was in the bathroom. Again, even a paranoid, who fears an intruder has got into his pitch dark home with the intention of murdering him, would rather not move an inch forward, fearing he would bump into the former, and wait for the beams of a flashlight or some sound he would make while groping his way into the room to start firing. One would expect Pistorius to at least wait behind a wall for the individual in the toilet to open its door and show up before firing four shots through a locked door into a small toilet cubicle from which there was no escape. Pistorius repeatedly told the court that all he was anxious about after hearing the suspicious noise was to protect Reeva, in which case he should have crosschecked by calling out to her before firing the deadly shots. In that prestigious court case, common sense was clearly the loser.

'Similarly, you have this sensational crime thriller *The Da Vinci Code* which took the world by storm a few years ago. The murder of the curator of Louvre Museum is the foundation on which the plot of the mystery-detective novel is built. The curator is shot by an intruder and he convulses and dies, lying in the position of Leonardo Da Vinci's *Vitruvian Man* with one of his fingers pointing towards Da Vinci's Madonna hanging on a wall. How on earth can a man who convulses and dies end up lying in a delineated straight-line posture of the *Vitruvian Man*? Dan Brown took all the crime thriller critics who lavished encomiums on the book and all the millions who read it for a ride with his flamboyant style of storytelling. *The New York Times* even went thus far: "Wow... Blockbuster Perfection..." Here again common sense was the loser.

'How similar are these stories to the one going the round about the great Einstein. The inventor of General Relativity had a cat as his favourite pet and the cat had a kitten, as usually is the case. Whenever the cat and the kitten wanted to play with Einstein, they would paw at the door of his room and he would readily open it for them. But that soon became too much of disturbance for his work. So he called the caretaker and asked him to provide a big hole for the mother cat and a small hole for the kitten in the door so that they could get in and go out as and when they liked without him having to get up and open the door for them each time.

'There have been many such cases, imagined and real, of brilliant minds bypassing common sense. I fervently hope and pray the poor garbage collector will not find himself at the receiving end of a similar miscarriage of common sense by legal luminaries. There is nothing more I need to do or can do for him.

'And as for desecration of the holy veil of which I may be held guilty, I vehemently object to the charge. How can I be held guilty of desecrating something I didn't then consider sacred? How can I be held guilty of misusing a thing whose every use is for me a misuse?'

At the break of dawn, a salvific ray of hope flashed on my mind. I'll undertake the Hajj and find relief from the mental torture by obtaining absolution of all my sins, provided, of course, the police won't have second thoughts and take the investigation to my door in the meanwhile.' Thankfully, the newspaper report hadn't said anything about the gold goblet I had placed along with Mrs Murari's jewellery in the waste basket.

Chapter - 10

The Call Of Jihad

On my return home, the first thing I did was to go and meet Murari. There was deep pain written on his face in the form of grey stubble, lifeless eyes and shaggy hair. After I offered him my condolences and he reciprocated with a warm embrace, we thought aloud on the tragic death of Mrs Murari.

"What is Baba's opinion on the police version of her death?" I asked.

"Baba says the police have got it perfectly right," he replied. "But I still have my doubts."

"The Baba can't be wrong."

"The garbage collector's wife came and met me the

other day," Murari explained. "Swearing on the head of the babe she was holding in her arms, she said her husband was being punished for being honest. According to her version, her husband found the jewellery while he was unloading the garbage from his vehicle to the garbage dump. He brought them home, wanting to hide and sell them secretly in instalments at a later date. It was at her insistence that he handed them over to the police. She claims that, instead of being rewarded for a good act, her husband is now booked for murder. She was begging me to believe her and press the police to find the real murderer. She sounded very genuine."

"Haven't all the lost jewellery been found?" I asked. "If the police were playing foul, they would also have siphoned off much of it."

"All the jewellery has been accounted for."

"That vouches for the honesty of the policemen who are handling the case."

"I do not doubt their honesty. They also have an additional item, a gold goblet. They found it while searching the area where her body was found. And the garbage collector's wife handed over to me another gold goblet, which was the only item she allowed her husband to keep as a concession to get him around to handover the jewellery to the police. Both the goblets smell of poison. Isn't that intriguing, Shreeman?"

"Of course it is," I bolted out. "Did you hand over the

gold goblet to the police?"

"I haven't," he answered. "I was waiting for the possibility of having this conversation with you before handing it over to them. Shreeman, my soul is in throes. This coincidence of my wife's death and the accident that left you unconscious shook the life out of me. The doctors weren't much hopeful that you would regain consciousness, but that miracle has happened, offering me a chance to confide in someone I can trust. I direly need your help."

"You can trust me to help you in whatever possible way I can."

"Please promise me you'll not share with anyone, including Shakeela, the secret thoughts I want to unburden."

"You have my word for it," I promised. "Nothing that you tell me will be shared with anyone."

"Even if, God forbid, something sours our friendship in the future?"

"Even if, heaven forbid, we become enemies through a vicious turn of fate."

"I have reasons to believe that my wife cheated on me. She didn't step out of home that fateful day, wearing the same dress and jewellery I bought for her for our silver jubilee celebration, to watch a test match. She was enjoying a secret relationship with someone. The postmortem report says she was six weeks pregnant. The two gold goblets are the last pieces in the puzzle. Her death was a suicide pact that went awry. For cheating on me, she got repaid by getting cheated on by her paramour. Both held a goblet each filled with poison. She drank, but he didn't. He threw her into the trench and rushed back to the city."

He and Shakeela were floating similar theories, but, unlike Shakeela, he seemed to think the culprit was someone other than the garbage collector. Was he hinting a fresh investigation was on the cards? If that ever happened, I was sure to get exposed. I had foreseen the danger that the missing goblet posed to me, but it had never crossed my mind the same was true of the foetus in Mrs Murari's womb. 'My dear parakeet, wherever you are, please come flying to my rescue.'

"So you suspect she was having an illicit affair with the garbage collector?"

"It doesn't make a difference to me who her paramour was. And I don't want to see him punished for engineering her death. In fact, I'm grateful to him for it. He spared me the obligation of dirtying my hands with her blood. It was after exerting political influence through Baba that the police have held back from investigating the case further. That she was murdered for theft of the jewellery suits me right: Me and my children will not have to carry the stigma of her illicit affaire. My only worry is about a poor garbage collector getting punished for a crime he may not have committed and the real culprit getting away undiscovered."

"Getting the DNA of the foetus tested and matching it with the DNA of the garbage collector would have solved his side of the mystery," I suggested.

"If you're willing to help, we can solve the entire mystery without much ado."

'Solve the entire mystery? He is completely off-track for that.'

"How do you want me to help?"

"Just own up the crime," he said, smirking.

"Which crime?" I barked.

"On your wife's request, I got your car repaired and serviced last week," he said, in a matter-of-fact tone. "Its backseat smelled of poison, the same poison the gold goblets smelled of."

I went blue. Some leftover poison from the goblet Mrs Murari used must have fallen on the backseat. The game was up for me.

After a prolonged wordy battle, which saw sallies of accusations and counter accusations that laid bare the beast in me and the Mammon in him, the encounter ended with Murari agreeing to keep my role in his wife's death a secret in return for a promise from me that I would keep all I knew about his ill-gotten wealth a secret. The innocent garbage collector would end up as the scapegoat driven to the prison, carrying all our sins.

The next day, Murari walked into my apartment, clean shaven and pearly eyed. Shakeela welcomed him with a radiant smile that sent a spear through my heart.

"Tragedies reveal a man's true quality," she said, gazing at him. "Only a man who believes Allah ordains everything for our good can take so terrible a tragedy as well as you have. It's so exhilarating to see you back in your old self."

"I drew strength mostly from the comforting words you had for me even as you were going through a great ordeal yourself," Murari reciprocated.

"Actually, I was feeling so bad that all I could do was to make a few phone calls," Shakeela said.

"But, more than anything else, those phone calls held me back from sinking into despair," Murari crooned. "I was planning to shift to a new spacious bungalow on Mahatma Gandhi Road, but I've dropped that idea now. A neighbour like you is more precious to me than the comforts of a palatial bungalow."

Weren't they telling me in my face that they have become sweethearts to repay me in my own coin?

"I thought you were putting up with the discomforts of your two-bedroom apartment for reasons of *vaastu*," I butted in.

"I had thought it was a secret only my wife and I knew," Murari said, making a wry face. "The *vaastu* advantage of the apartment was linked to the star of my wife. It has ceased with her death."

"I heard your relatives have already made arrangements for your second marriage," I said. "How thoughtful they are."

"They want me to marry a second cousin who is just a couple years older than my eldest daughter," Murari explained. "There's no question of me agreeing to that marriage or any other. I already have had all the joys and sorrows marriage can bring in one life. From now on, I prefer to get lost in love than in marriage. Baba has taught me to take love beyond the bond of marriage. Besides, bringing in a wife now is sure to cause emotional strain to my children. They are my first priority now."

The doorbell rang. It was Rukmani, Murari's second daughter.

"Grandpa and grandma have come, papa," Rukmani announced, standing at the door.

"They have come to press for the marriage," Murari said, rising to go. "This time around, I'll make sure they won't bring it up ever again."

"Shakeela, I'm seriously thinking of buying a more spacious apartment in Nehru *Nagar*," I said, after he left. "There's something seriously wrong with the *vaastu* of our apartment complex. We have been moving from crisis to crisis since the day we started living in it."

"Who doesn't face crises in life, dear," Shakeela

admonished. "Look at the way Mr Murari faces them. You're forgetting that we have also won a ten million lottery after we made this apartment our home. Would this thought have come to you if we didn't have that money? As it is, this apartment is comfortable enough for us. I'm going to feel out of place in a posh locality like Nehru *Naga*r. Who knows if I'll get there a neighbour like Mr Murari to be of some assistance? You can't imagine the troubles he took to search for our son when he went missing."

"But how often will he be available here to be of help to you?" I retorted. "It was by a rare coincidence that he happened to be available here when our son went missing. Now that he is a widower, he will spend all his time with Baba at his ashram."

"He told me last evening that he will spend only weekends with Baba now on. He requested me to have an eye on the children during his absence. That's one more reason for us to stay on here. Don't we owe at least that much to Mr Murari?"

I kept mum, leaving it to her to interpret my silence for a yes or a no. Whichever way she took it, I for one, concluded that I had lost her forever to my archenemy. How I wished I had drunk the goblet of poison Mrs Murari had offered me so lovingly.

"I'll just go and offer my condolences to Mr Murari's parents," Shakeela said. "I didn't have a chance to meet them after the death of their daughter-in-law."

She then rose and shuffled towards the entrance door. I decided then and there to clandestinely install webcams in my house and have them connected to my smartphones. I got the job done a day before I started attending office, after sending off Shakeela and the children to my mother-in-law for the weekend. But, torn between attending to my work and following Shakeela's movements on the smartphone, my nerves got shredded.

And there she is opening the door for Murari. She doesn't even wait for the door to close before grabbing and kissing him. 'How shameless of you, Shakeela!' Off they go into the bedroom. He undresses her, and she him. It's Shakeela pushing him on, just as Mrs Murari did with me. Copycat vengeance. His mouth is invading her all over. They are rolling on my bed, twined like mating snakes. I can stand it no more. I rush down to the car park. My car roars away, jumping signals and leaping over closed railway gates until it screeches to a halt in front of the stairway leading to my apartment. I ring the doorbell of my house, but the door doesn't open for many agonising minutes. Desperate, I kick at the door with all my might. The door refuses to open, vibrating mockingly. I rush down to my car and fetch the wheel spanner. I succeed in shattering a bottom panel of the door with it. As I squeeze myself through the opening, I can hear Shakeela's love groans. "Stop it!" I shriek. I storm into the bedroom and pluck Murari off Shakeela. "Bloody bitch!" I scream, and rain blows on her with the wheel spanner. She writhes in pain, and then, of a sudden, pounces on me. I pin her down, but she gives me a ferocious push and I fall off the bed, hitting my head hard against the floor.

A few seconds passed before I could distinguish between dream and reality.

When I woke up, Shakeela was raising my head and placing it on her lap.

"Yah Allah!" she wailed, rubbing down the bulge on my head. "What's the matter? Had a bad dream?"

I was at a loss to reply.

The children came running. My daughter switched on all the lights. Then the three helped me rise and get into bed.

A phone call from Shakeela brought Murari to the scene immediately. Shakeela explained to him that I hit her repeatedly on the head and then rolled out of bed. She then showed him the bulge on my head.

"We'll take him to the hospital." Shakeela said.

"I have come ready for that," Murari said, taking out a car key from his pants pocket.

"Hospital?" I asked. "For what?"

"Lie quiet, dear," Shakeela pleaded, rubbing down the bulge on my head. "You have had a terrible fall. Didn't the doctor tell you to be careful about even shaking your head?"

"I'm okay," I said.

"It looks like your brain is suffering the aftershocks of the accident," Murari said, referring to the fall that sent me into a coma. "It's dangerous to take a chance,"

"There's nothing of the sort," I protested. "I'll be okay after a good sleep."

All the four of them pretended not to hear me and literally carried me into Murari's car. In twenty minutes, I was back in the hospital I had left less than a week back.

ꙮ

After carefully studying the sequence of events that brought me back to the hospital, the doctors came to the conclusion that I was disoriented for the very reason Murari had suggested. They impressed upon Shakeela and me that, more than anything else, I needed an atmosphere of mental peace to absorb the aftershocks that may last for a couple of months. One of the doctors suggested yoga and meditation as reliable means to achieve it. Oh, if only I could tell them nothing in the world would bring me peace of mind unless and until Murari was banished to some remote part of the globe where he would be untraceable for Shakeela!

ꙮ

There was no question of Shakeela agreeing to the use of a diabolically un-Islamic method like yoga. But she was in frantic search for an alternative. She found one by the time

I was discharged from the hospital after a week – a mullah who had gained great renown as an exorcist of evil Jinn. In the morning of the day after I reached back home from the hospital, she took me to Mullah Omar.

A bearded old man took me to Mullah Omar who was seated in a room having walls covered with verses from the Quran. A mesmeric smile cresting over a long flowing beard drew me instantly to his mystic aura.

"What's troubling you, son?" asked the Mullah.

That endearing tone of his opened the floodgates of my racked brain. Everything that I have till now described, from the fateful journey I made during a total solar eclipse in search of a cure for kidney stones to the dream I had about Murari and Shakeela making love on my bed, gushed out in a non-stop confession. The assessment he made of the twists of fate I had gone through gave me the impression that he was a very learned man in subjects both profane and Islamic and that my frankness had won him over. After spending quite some time studying my face, hands and nails, he finally arrived at the conclusion that I was possessed by a female jinn.

He then bid me lie down on the floor, which I promptly did. He bent down and recited quranic verses in my ears until my eyelids began to close. Then he placed headphones on my ears. With eyes closed, I listened to the Islamic chants and ethereal sounds that came through them. After about half an hour, he held my eyelids apart and puts some drops into my eyes. So excruciating was the pain they caused that I rolled on the floor, bawling like a child. After the pain subsided, he bid me rise and sit leaning against a wall. He then gave me a glass of bitter concoction to drink. As the drink travelled down my throat, I began losing control over my body. I started swaying. Soon the swaying became violent and I began to growl and hiss. Two men then came holding green coloured whips. They competed with each other in flogging me. Screaming, I ran for the door. I came against Mullah Omar, who pushed me back. Lashes rained on me as I tore around and around the room. I sought an end to the torment by wilfully tottering and slumping to the floor. It worked. The whipping ceased. Mullah Omar stood over me and yelled, "Leave him! Leave him!" I lay motionless. "Leave him if you don't want to be whipped again!!" the mullah shrieked. I realised I had to do something that will signal to him that the jinn was leaving me. I rolled on the floor, going round and round, imitating my daughter who had as a suckling attracted Kali worshippers on a city road margin. It too worked. The whippers lifted me by the hand and sat me leaning against a wall. The mullah then inserted two fingers deep into my gullet. I vomited into a basin held by the whippers. The process got repeated thrice, after which I became lifeless with exhaustion. Soon, the cadence of quranic chanting lulled me to sleep. I had terrifying dreams in which fighter cocks attacked me from all sides with their spurs, wild beasts tore me apart, a female jinn sliced off my penis and ate it raw. When I woke up some ten hours later, I was lying in my bed, tended by Shakeela and soothed by quranic recitation flowing from the surround sound system I had installed in the bedroom a few months back.

Drained of even the barest strength to resist, I submitted then on to a daily visit to Mullah Omar. For eight weeks I underwent every variation of Islamically sanctioned exorcist rites, except whipping. On each visit, I was given a list of prayers I should recite and a bottle of water made holy by the mullah's prayers, which alone I was to drink. The water would, I was told, seep into every part of my body and render it uninhabitable for jinn for all time to come. And all this while, quranic recitation followed me twenty-four seven. In the end, I became a ball of malleable dough which Mullah Omar could turn into any shape he liked.

The first thing he turned me into was a whipping assistant for exorcising jinn from a woman. I played my part so well that the woman was carried off as a lump of flesh in less than fifteen minutes. I felt elated by the achievement. In the hands of Mullah Omar, I had become a worthy instrument of Allah.

After the exorcism of the woman had crossed five continuous sessions, Mullah Omar divulged to me her identity. She was the wife of the garbage collector. Infuriated by her commitment to honesty, an evil jinn had taken possession of her. The jinn threw her into bouts of hysteria. The information brought me briefly back into my old self, a normal remorseful individual who felt deeply about making others suffer for the consequences of one's sins.

"A crime I committed is causing terrible suffering to innocent people," I said. "How can I get redemption from the guilt that is gnawing at me?"

"The guilt of it is bound to follow you all your life," Mullah Omar said. "And even if you escape punishment in this life for the crime, Allah is sure to punish you for it in the afterlife."

"Will I be sent to hell?"

"Yes, to the hottest part of hell."

"And suppose I confess to my crime and suffer punishment for it in this life?"

"There is no need of that," Mullah Omar comforted. "Allah has in his mercy and goodness provided a means by which we can not only find redemption from guilt and eternal punishment for all our sins, from the smallest to the gravest, but also to get a rich reward in heaven."

I had little doubt he was referring to the hajj.

"I know whoever goes on the hajj and performs it in the right spirit will return as a newborn, free from all sins," I said. "I have decided to go on the hajj at the earliest opportunity."

"And what does the hajj mean for you?" the mullah asked.

"The holy hajj will cleanse me of all my sins and save me from Allah's punishment."

"You're repeating yourself," the mullah admonished. "As a recent convert to Islam, you're yet to understand the true significance of the hajj. One of the main rites performed during the hajj is sacrificing a sheep, which commemorates Prophet Ibrahim's willingness to offer his son Ishmael as a sacrifice to Allah. If you perform the hajj, you'll only find absolution of all your sins, but if you're willing to kill even the dearest loved one of yours for the sake of Allah as Prophet Ibrahim did and if you are willing to die for the sake of Allah as Ishmael did, you'll be rewarded with immense riches, a palace grander than any you can imagine and seventy-two angelic virgins in the afterlife."

For me, who was thirsting for deliverance from the torment of remorse, that was a stupendous promise, and an irresistible temptation. But I wanted to make sure it wasn't a mirage.

"But a mullah had once warned during an Eid al-Adha sermon against interpreting Ibrahim's sacrifice as a licence to kill," I said. "He said we should instead imitate the prophet's willingness to give up what is most precious for us for the sake of Allah."

"He just taught you a watered down version, which is not going to help you find salvation," the mullah warned. "Don't forget you have on your hands the blood of a woman and on your head the curse of an innocent man and his family who are suffering the consequences of it. To obtain the forgiveness of Allah and the joys of heaven, you'll have to make the ultimate sacrifice."

"What is it?"

"Jihad!" He thundered. "Dying and killing for the faith! Dying and killing for the glory of Allah! Dying and killing for conquering the world for Allah!"

"Whom should I kill and how should I die?"

"You should kill every infidel who refuses to convert and every unfaithful Muslim who deviates from the Holy Quran," he said. "And I shall teach you how to die doing it."

Despite Mullah Omar's charisma, it took some time for me to digest the idea of killing to please Allah, because I was under the impression that mankind had long ago progressed beyond the days of human sacrifice. In my own country, anyone who killed a fellow human being to propitiate Kali would be booked for murder and sent to the gallows. I had also recently learnt that a man had been charged with murder for performing human sacrifice for finding a hidden treasure. Mullah Omar was taking me back to the primitive times of human sacrifice and also asking me to perform it to find a hidden treasure in the afterlife. But the Mullah won the day in the end. He persuaded me to realise that, from the day I stepped out of home during a total solar eclipse, I had travelled back in time to the days of the early man who fashioned God in his own image as one who fed on the flesh and blood of animals and men. I had to become a primitive man to find an escape from the hell that the modern world had become and in which I was trapped. 'Thank you, Allah, for this revelation that, that humanitarian trip I made on a solar eclipse day has finally led me to true salvation. I shall kill and die for Your sake, in the manner Your chosen one, Mullah Omar, decides for me. If I may make a small request, I am not very particular about getting the grandest palace in heaven, but please reserve the most beautiful virgins for me.'

Mullah Omar gave me a pamphlet titled *The Best Way to Die* to read in the foolproof secrecy of his home. In reality, the book explained many ways of the best way to die.

1. Join a squad that will storm the holy Kaaba two years from now and kill as many of the hajjis as possible. It is planned as retaliation for the hajj sermon that denounced the holy war jihadists are fighting in Iraq and Syria for establishing a caliphate that will, Insha Allah, extend to the entire world in less than ten years. The jihadists will perform the hajj in all its purity and attack the hajjis while performing the final circumambulation of the Kaaba. A

disgruntled Saudi prince whom Allah has inspired to join the caliphate movement will make AK-47s available to the fighters at the nick of time.

A very attractive offer: hajj and jihad at one stroke.

2. Fly to Turkey and cross over to Syria under cover of darkness, wearing a black veil, and join the ISIS fighters there. There, one can enjoy the pleasure of spraying bullets on lined-up captured men or shooting them in the head one after another, of sacrificing children, re-enacting the aborted sacrifice of Ishmael over a hundred times and more, and of raping women. One can also graduate to an exclusive club of jihadists who are chosen for world fame by beheading an American or British hostage for the benefit of Facebook and Google viewers.

A forbidding option at first sight, but, on second thought, requires a very advanced stage of jihadist fervour.

3. Cross over to Pakistan through Kashmir and join the Lashkar-e-Taiba, which is plotting to spirit away A Q Khan, the father of Pakistan's nuclear bomb, and hand him over to the ISIS. A massive mobilisation of ten thousand jihadi fighters from LeT, Pak Taliban and ISIS is under way for staging the daring operation. One could become part of the group that storms A Q Khan's residence in overwhelming numbers, or of the group that provides a long safe passage for the convoy that will take the scientist through land and sea to ISIS territory through rebel controlled Syria. The

project is the brain child of a former chief of Pakistan's ISI, who has promised the Lashkar-e-Taiba that the first nuclear bomb thus produced will be dropped on India's Parliament House using a captured Pakistani launcher.

It was an ambitious project that could ultimately clear the world of all Infidels and take all believers to heaven as soon as it reached fruition, but the risks involved and the gestation time it required could keep me in my miserable existence longer than I could bear.

4. Become a member of an elite group that will stage a suicide attack on the Prime Minister of India at the residence of Satguru Murdan, whom unfailingly he visits on the first of every month to receive blessings. Mullah Omar is getting a 300 metre tunnel dug for the purpose from the official residence of a Member of Parliament, whom he has won over to the jihadist cause, to the compound of the Satguru. The attack will be a night operation that will coincide with the completion of the tunnel, which will, Insha Allah, happen within nine months .

This appeared to be the most attractive choice.

I took only an hour to digest the contents of the report and get back to Mullah Omar.

"Which of the four missions would you want to take

part in?" the mullah asked.

"I'm willing for any that you may assign, mullah," I replied.

"No special preference?"

"The fourth one looks more attractive," I replied.

"For you, I have a fifth one in mind," the mullah declared. "It's a mission that none but you can best accomplish."

"All praise to Allah for choosing me for such a privileged mission!"

"You'll have to accomplish it singlehandedly," the mullah said.

"All thanks to Allah for making me his chosen one!"

He then explained the details of the mission. The *shastipoorthi* celebration of Satsang Baba was due in six months. People in their thousands were expected to flock from all over the world to Baba's ashram for the occasion. I would have to get infected with Ebola virus and go for the night *darshans* of the Baba ten days prior to the *sashtipoorthi* day. Baba's devotees would have a once-in-life chance to embrace His Holiness on the occasion. That would ensure the spread of the deadly infection to the entire world and the death of all infidels and unfaithful believers. In all probability, I might die and be chosen for the joys of heaven, but all the other soldiers of Allah would be saved by the protective measures that would have been put in place for them by that time in Caliphate territory. A new world where only true worshippers of Allah lived would thus emerge in a very short time.

What a great opportunity to wreak vengeance on Baba for using me as his plaything; On Murari, whom Baba would embrace, for cheating on me; and on Shakeela, whom Murari would embrace, for paying me back in kind! But I had to save my children. Love for them was one of the two slender connections I still had to my old self and the world of ordinary humans. The other was the remorse I still felt when the garbage collector's wife visited Mullah Omar for the exorcistic sessions. After expressing exhilaration at being chosen for a mission that would transform the world to the Kingdom of Allah, I shared those concerns with Mullah Omar.

"You leave those to me," the mullah assured. "I shall make arrangements to shift your children to a protective environment before the Ebola epidemic starts breaking out from Baba's ashram. I shall also hire the best lawyer to represent the garbage collector in the case. I shall tell his wife about it on her next visit, which I hope will be the last."

It would surely be the woman's last visit to the mullah, because the jinn would definitely leave her the moment she gets the offer from him. In any case, thanks to Mullah Omar's promise on both counts, I was at peace and ready for the divine mission Allah had exclusively chosen me for.

ꙮ

Even as Mullah Omar was arranging for me a trip to Sierra Leon for getting infected with Ebola, instruction came from ISIS headquarters that it wasn't necessary. Instead, Mullah Omar would get a hand-delivered parcel containing a safe sealed Ebola infected cloth piece. I would only have to wipe my face with it to get infected.

ꙮ

I am in the last days of a very eventful sojourn on earth. I am attending duty regularly. I no more plunge into nightmares about Murari sneaking into my bedroom in my absence. At home I have become a very devout Muslim, and when Murari comes home from Baba's ashram, I go and substitute him for Baba's night darshan. I have become a more loveable person than ever before to everyone around. When the jihadi fervour gets hold of you, you become a lamb – for leading wolves to slaughter.

Shakeela has gone with the children to visit her mother. I will get the webcams removed from my house before she returns in the evening. I want to sport a beard and a scull cap like Mullah Omar, and I also very much want to paint my house green and purge it of TV, refrigerator, ariconditioner and every other luxury item, but the thought that it may lead to my jihadi intention getting revealed is holding me back.

I don't expect anything very eventful to happen before I leave for Baba's ashram for the last time tomorrow. I shall add an epitaph for me below. Mullah Omar has promised to upload this veil stricken story of my life on his website on the day of my martyrdom.

Epitaph:

Here lies a man for whom life was a veil,
As dark as a total solar eclipse.